A
Harlequin
Romance

OTHER
Harlequin Romances
by BELINDA DELL

Many of these titles are available at your local bookseller,
or through the Harlequin Reader Service.

For a free catalogue listing all available Harlequin Romances,
send your name and address to:

HARLEQUIN READER SERVICE,
M.P.O. Box 707, Niagara Falls, N.Y. 14302
Canadian address: Stratford, Ontario, Canada.

or use order coupon at back of book.

LOVELY IS THE ROSE

by

BELINDA DELL

HARLEQUIN BOOKS   TORONTO
WINNIPEG

Original hard cover edition published in 1973
by Mills & Boon Limited.

© Belinda Dell 1973

SBN 373-01749-9

Harlequin edition published January 1974

Printed in Canada

1749

CHAPTER ONE

AS they jolted along the stony track Corinne realized that this really was "rough country". All around them lay the moors, rolling in splendour to the hills where spring rain-clouds were casting patches of shadow over the short grass cropped by sheep that looked, from the distance, like little clumps of daisies.

The Land-Rover went over a particularly deep rut. Corinne gave a stifled cry and grabbed the side of the vehicle.

"Too much for you?" asked Travers, cutting down the speed a little.

"No, no! It's exhilarating, really. But you were right when you warned me it was wild up here." She watched in amazement as a bird rose, calling, from the heather. "What was that?"

"No idea." He pointed ahead and to the left. "That's where the motorway is to run, along the side of that hill above the little river."

Corinne followed the line of his pointing hand. She saw a gentle slope where water glinted here and there, like a ribbon hidden among the bushes. A faint white haze seemed to lie over the green of the bushes; she thought it was probably some sort of blossom. A pretty spot ... It was a pity it would all have to go for the sake of the motorway.

The motorway was what had brought her here, in-directly. Corinne Lenwood was secretary to the chief engineer of Eldin Consultants, owned by the father of the man who was now driving her through this wide empty stretch of the Scottish Borders. Travers had come to supervise the work of the firm's surveying team which was making a preliminary study on behalf of the Ministry of Highways, and to set up an area office in Hawick, largest of the Border towns.

"It's a prosperous neighbourhood," Mr. Eldin had said, "with a lot of new building likely to take place. Just the spot for a branch of our firm."

So here they were. Travers Eldin had come north two days ago and had done a litte groundwork—got a list of available office premises, introduced himself to one or two influential people, and booked himself into an agreeable hotel in a village some ten miles south of Hawick. That was where they were heading now; this detour to see the survey team was simply to give Corinne a glimpse of the countryside.

She was impressed, no doubt about it. City-bred and city-loving, she'd really had no idea there was still so much empty space in Britain. She kept reading in the papers how everything was becoming built-up, yet here was this vast, empty countryside, intensely green in the valleys and heather-clad on the hills, and peopled—so far as she could see—only by sheep. Now and again she had glimpsed a ruined tower on a vantage point, but modern habitations were few and far between; since Travers collected her off the train at Berwick the journey seemed to be taking them deeper and deeper into a sort of landscape-painting.

The April breeze was fresh. She huddled closer into her pale pink suede coat, her dark tawny hair catching on its collar. She wished she had brought a woolly scarf. Still, this was the country for buying woolly scarves, with the River Tweed itself only a couple of miles away!

"Cold?" asked Travers.

"A bit," she admitted. "It must be chilly for the men working out here, Trav?"

"Oh, they're used to it. They've got good thick jackets. No, it's not the cold that bothers them, it's the occasional mists that come down on them out of nowhere. A bit difficult to see a surveying pole twenty yards away when visibility's down to five!"

"It sounds jolly." She gave him a quick glance in which there was some veiled anxiety. "Are you sure you're going to like it here, Trav?"

"Of course, darling. It's going to be great to do things on my own, without Dad breathing down my neck."

She took his arm and gave it a sympathetic squeeze. Working for the firm as she did, she had daily examples of how Trav had to fight for his independence. Norman Eldin, his father, was in many ways a remarkable, an admirable man : coming out of the Army when he was no longer young, he had used his Royal Engineers training to set up a consultancy business—that was to say, he didn't undertake any construction, but investigated and advised on possibilities.

Travers Eldin was the heir apparent to this business. After gaining an engineering degree he had taken on a lot of the work. But Norman seemed unable to accept the fact that his son was a grown man with the qualifications of an expert. Time and again he lifted things from Trav's hands at the first sign of problems—problems which, Corinne was sure, Trav could have solved for himself if left alone.

But here in the Borders it would all be different. Norman Eldin was safely left in London, while Trav

7

made a new beginning both for the firm and for his own life.

Corinne watched him unnoticed as he guided the Land-Rover over the uneven surface of the moorland track. He was an exceptionally attractive man, dark, tanned, and rather elegant in his brown trenchcoat with the collar turned up against the breeze. She often wondered why he wasn't already married—goodness knows, women gathered round him at every social event. She suspected that, once again, his father was the reason : Mr. Eldin wanted his son to "marry well".

She sighed to herself. That more or less disposed of *her* chances. Mr. Eldin was never going to approve of a daughter-in-law whose ancestral home was a semi-detached in Wembley and whose fortune consisted of a few pieces of attractive costume jewellery and a wardrobe full of fashionable clothes.

Corinne was a good secretary and earned good money, but she tended to spend it as soon as she got it. She liked to get out and about—parties, discos, musical shows at the theatre or cinema. Clothes were something of a passion with her; she would cheerfully admit that she owned eight coats. Any girl who shared a flat with Corinne was lucky—she was quite capable of giving away a dress after wearing it only a couple of times.

What was a girl like Corinne doing in the wilds of the Borders? Staying close to the man she loved—what else? She could have resigned from her job as Travers Eldin's secretary when he decided to come north; without difficulty she could have found a post as good, if not better, in London where all her friends were. But no—some things are more important than going to first nights or dancing at the latest "in" place.

So here she was, being taken to see the survey team

in the midst of a vast expanse of heather, most un-suitably clad in a coat of fine suede with shoes to match, while above her the white clouds scudded in a pale blue sky and the larks sang in thanksgiving for spring.

When Trav drew up at the surveying site, the men turned with pleasure at the interruption—a pleasure doubled when they saw the tall slim figure being helped down from the vehicle. The brisk air had brought colour to her fine skin and a sparkle to her grey eyes. She smiled in enjoyment of their admiration, but after a while, when they started to talk technicalities, began to feel left out.

It occurred to her that the bushes she had seen from the track must be over the shoulder of the hill. She would like to know what they were ... So off she strolled, up the slope and along a steep path, through a little gulley, and then to the bank of the stream.

The bushes turned out to be wild roses, still in bud, growing low against the ground on spiny stems. Try as she might to pick one, the thorns made it impossible. She tried approaching the thicket from several angles, unaware as she walked that she was going uphill and that the rain clouds were drifting down from the summit towards her.

Almost as dramatically as a curtain falling, the mist came down around her. She turned, blinking in sur-prise. "Oh, bother!" she muttered. "Now which is the way back?"

Whichever way it was, she had very little choice. The spiny shrubs of the rose thicket seemed to be almost everywhere, so that if she wanted to make any progress it would have to be towards the heather. She made her way slowly, peering ahead into the greyness. She really couldn't understand how, from one moment to the next, visibility could be cut to almost nothing. Now she understood why Trav had said the surveying team found the mist such a handicap.

All at once a figure started up in front of her, literally from the ground at her feet.

Corinne gave a stifled shriek of terror and stepped back. Her foot caught in a tussock. She went over backwards in a sprawling heap.

"Whit a de'il—?" exclaimed a man's voice. "Wha's there?"

"Oh! Now *look* what you've done—" She broke off, scrambling to her feet.

A strong, large hand grasped her to help her up. "Are ye a' richt?" asked the man. "Ye came doon an awfu' skelp."

None of this made any sense to Corinne. He might as well have been talking Urdu. She said, slowly and distinctly as the British do when talking to foreigners, "You gave me a fright. Do you know this district? Are you a..." A what? What would be the occupation of a man out in these hills? "Are you a shepherd, my man?" she ended.

She heard a stifled sound that might have been either a laugh or a cough. "You're surely an English lassie?" he said, obviously making an effort to speak more clearly. "What are you doing up by the Burneybank?"

"The what? To tell the truth I'm not very sure where I am. I was with some people, but I wandered off."

"That's not a very sensible thing to be doing here abouts, missie. Ye could end up by falling either into the burn or into the thornbauk."

"Into the thornbauk? Oh, you mean those rose bush things."

"Aye, those. A sheep that gets catchit in there can

stay for a day and a night unless somebody comes along to set him free."

"Dear me! Then I'm glad I didn't get caught. Could you tell me how to get back to the track in the valley, below the stream?"

"Ye'd best bide here till the haar clears."

"Till when? I'm afraid I don't quite follow, my good man."

"Och, sair's ma heart to hear it!" He broke off—it occurred to her that perhaps the fog had got into his throat. When he resumed it was to give her a long list of directions she was quite unable to understand because he had relapsed into the Border dialect again.

"Well, thank you ever so much," she said politely when he finished, although he hadn't been the slightest help to her. "I think I'd better just stay here a bit."

"I doot ye canna be as douce as your voice," remarked her helper. "Ye ha'e the lilt o' a throssel."

"Really?" Corinne said, completely baffled.

At that moment the capricious wind swept the cloud off the hillside, and she found herself facing a tall young man in a thick Fair Isle sweater and jeans. The mischievous grin on his face vanished as quickly as the mist.

"I'm thinking noo ye'll be able to find your freens," he remarked, pointing with solemnity down the slope to his left. "If ye just daunder doon there, ye'll come on the path."

She caught enough of this to realize he was telling her which direction to take. She also had a very strong impression he was laughing at her. She studied him; he certainly wasn't her idea of a shepherd, because he had no shepherd's crook and no sheepdog. Besides, he wasn't old and weathered, as a shepherd ought to be—he looked to be in his early thirties, very fit and muscular, with a bony face under a thatch of careless fairish brown hair.

Now that she was able to take a good look at him, she saw that he had a thick, somewhat battered book under his arm, and a pocket lens in his hand. There was something "learned" about both of them.

"Are you ... are you a scientist?" she enquired.

He shook his head.

"But you're not a shepherd?"

"I sell agricultural machinery for a living, and go out botanizing as a hobby. My name's Duncan Donaldson."

"*Oh*," she exclaimed with indignation. "And all that gobbledygook—?"

"Gobbledygook?" he echoed, laughing. "I'll have you know that was Lallands—Lowland Scots, a very fine, expressive language still alive and well and being used hereabouts. I'm sorry if it puzzled you. I simply couldn't resist it when you came over all English-aristocratic with me."

"But you talked in that funny way when we first came on each other—"

"Yes, but that was because I thought you were a Borders lass. And it's *you* that talks in a funny way," he pointed out, his grey eyes teasing her. "Nobody else round here talks like that."

"You're impossible," she said, and turning on her heel, marched off.

"Excuse me, you're going the wrong way," he called.

She stopped short. Immediately he was at her elbow. "Don't be cross," he said. "Let me show you the path down to the valley, Miss—er?"

"I'll find my own way, thank you."

"You're walking straight back in among the burnets."

"The what?"

"The thorn bushes."

"They're roses," Corinne said. "I know a rose when I see it."

"Who's arguing with you?"

"But you called them something else."

"I called them by their name. What kind of roses are they, according to you?"

"What kind? Well . . . er . . , wild roses."

"Considering they're growing on an uncultivated hillside, you can't be far wrong. But there are about half a dozen different wild roses."

"Well then . . . they're dog-roses," she ventured, that being the only name that came to her.

"No, no. The dog-rose looks pink in the bud, and isn't common in Scotland. Those are burnet roses, the kind we find in sandy soil up here. I suppose if you've just arrived in the district you haven't heard of a village called Burney—"

"As a matter of fact, I have," she interrupted, because that was where she was going to stay.

"Oh, you have? Well, it gets its name from this rose because it grows so profusely around here. There you are—now you've had a lesson in botany and local history, all for free. Does that make amends for misbehaving?"

Despite herself, she relented. "I wonder how long it will take me to get acclimatized around here?" she observed as she fell into step beside him.

"You mean you're not just on holiday or passing through?"

"No, my firm's opening an office. I'll be living here for a while."

13

"Welcome to Burneybank. Another rose among the roses."

She blushed. "Oh . . . thank you . . ."

"But nevertheless," he said, pulling her by the arm so that she stopped in her tracks, "do be careful where you're putting your dainty little foot. That's a very rare flower you're about to trample to death."

Corinne stared down at the ground. All she saw was a clump of narrow leaves rather like those of a lily of the valley, but without blossoms.

"Are you pulling my leg again?"

"I'm quite serious."

"Well, what is it, then?" she said in disbelief.

"I haven't the slightest intention of telling you. The fewer people who know about it the better, otherwise we'll have picnickers coming up here to pull it up for their window-boxes."

He really was the most impossible man! "I couldn't care less about your plants," she said crossly. "If you'll just point out the path, I'll manage by myself."

"Just go down the brae. You don't mind if I do likewise? I'm on my way home."

"It's a free country."

"You never spoke a truer word. In this part of the world the very wind on the hills breathes the word 'freedom'. What does the wind say in your home town, Miss—?"

"In my home town you can't hear it because of the noise of the traffic," she confessed.

"You're from London?"

"There's traffic in other places besides London, but as a matter of fact, yes. I am a Londoner."

"You'll find it something of a contrast, living here."

This was undeniably true. The ground underfoot was

marshy now and her pale suede shoes were squelching in moisture, yet on her unprotected head the bright sun, having gained the better of the rain clouds, was beating down strongly. She couldn't remember ever meeting with such contrasting conditions in London.

"I suppose I'll get used to it," she said with some doubt in her tone.

"I hope you will. Careful just here." He put an arm around her to guide her through the soggy ground. "It's a bit precarious here—the spring comes up to the surface a little to the west and makes that little stream by the patch of burnet roses, but just for a hundred yards hereabouts you have to watch your footing."

He directed her from one clump of firm grass to the next, and all would have been well if Travers had not appeared unexpectedly round the side of some whin bushes.

"Hi, Corinne! So there you are!"

"I'm coming," Corinne called in reply, taking an unplanned and eager step.

Her foot went into muddy water up to the ankle. Grabbing at Duncan Donaldson for support, she pulled her foot free—leaving her shoe in the marsh.

"*Oh!*" She floundered wildly for an instant.

Next moment she was swept up in safety into a pair of strong arms. The brilliant blue, tan and white of the Fair Isle sweater dazzled her eyes. She felt the rough wool against her cheek.

She looked up. He was smiling down at her, as he moved swiftly to firmer ground.

"Oh . . . thank you . . . but I'm too heavy for you—"

" 'Strong are mine arms, and little care
A weight so slight as thine to bear.' "

he quoted. "Besides, you can't walk with only one shoe."

She said nothing more. It was oddly pleasant to be carried so lightly with her face pressed to his shoulder. A sensation took control of her—new, untasted, strangely tempting.

Trav's voice woke her from this strange momentary delirium. "What happened? Corinne, are you all right?"

"She left a shoe behind in the swamp," her knight errant explained. "I'll take her to your car, shall I?"

"Oh ... well ..." Trav seemed to hesitate. Yet it was hardly possible to hand her over to him like a parcel, nor could she manage with only one shoe. So Corinne was brought the remaining few yards to the Land-Rover, and gently deposited in the passenger seat.

"Too bad about the shoe," Duncan said. "I'll fish it out for you if you like, but it's never going to match that one." He nodded at the survivor, which in fact wasn't in a very good state either thanks to its encounter with the boggy ground.

"And they were new, too," Corinne mourned.

"It's not very good sense to go walking in Border country in a pair of thin suede shoes," he said with a complete lack of sympathy.

"Well ... er ... thanks very much," Trav said, letting in the clutch.

"A pleasure, I assure you." And to Corinne : "Goodbye, Cinderella."

"Goodbye."

"Who was *he*?" asked Trav as they lurched away down the track.

"I met him studying the plants through a pocket lens," Corinne said. "He got up all of a sudden right in front of me—scared me half to death. His name's Donaldson."

"Donaldson?"

"Yes, do you know it?"

"I expect it's a common name around here. But funnily enough Dad was saying that if we needed trucks and tractors, I could get them from a man called Donaldson."

"Then it's the same man! He told me he sold agricultural machinery."

"What a pity you didn't mention it, Corinne. I could have introduced myself."

She was about to protest that she couldn't possibly have known he wanted to introduce himself, but another thought took her attention instead. "Shall we be seeing much of him?"

"Why?" He gave her a frowning glance. "Don't you like him?"

"He's . . . rather an individualist."

"Oh, it takes all sorts . . . In any case he'll soon mend his manners when he finds we're bringing money his way."

"I'm not so sure," she murmured. But the words were lost in the crashing of gears as Trav negotiated the steep gradient down to the village of Burney.

The village astounded her. It was so very, very small. Somehow, since Travers had chosen a hotel here as temporary living quarters, she had expected something the size of a village in Surrey or Hertfordshire, the sort of places she was accustomed to go to when she left London for "a day in the country". But this community could surely number not more than five hundred souls to judge by the few houses, which were small, stone-built, and slate-roofed. They fronted straight on to the street, rather primly; but there were window-boxes full of spring bulbs, and down the little alleys she glimpsed back gardens, glowing with primula, early cyclamen, and camellia bushes. One or two of the gardens, she noticed, had tamed the spiny burnet rose to grow as a sort of hedge, speckled now with the soft cream of the buds.

They drove on through the only street, to the far side of the village. Here, sheltered by a well-wooded rise and facing south, stood what had once been a laird's mansion. A low wall with stone balustrades protected its lawn and shrubbery, through which the drive led in a graceful curve to the entrance, where a wrought-iron sign proclaimed "Burney House Hotel".

"You mean we're staying *here?*" Corinne gasped.

"Thought you'd like it," he said, with some amusement. "It's a three-star place, and the comfort has to be experienced to be believed."

"But, Trav—the cost must be enormous—"

"Not as much as you'd think. In any case, Dad said to spare no expense to get this new office properly established, so I'm taking him at his word."

She stared up at the crow-stepped gables, the tall sloping roof, the rounded turret-corners. "Is it very old?"

"Originally sixteenth century, I gather from the advertising brochure, but of course it's been added to and altered since then. Used to belong to Lord Caithdale, whoever he may have been—never heard of him, so he couldn't have been very important in Scottish history. Not like Bruce and the Black Douglas and such. Come on."

As they got out of the Land-Rover a porter appeared to take Corinne's luggage. She was framing a question about how a place so far off the beaten track could possibly make any money when, as she entered the hotel, she was presented with the answer. The porch was full of angler's equipment—rods in their long slender cases, baskets, folded umbrellas, waders. This was a centre for fishermen; she recalled the dozens of rushing, tumbling streams she had seen on her way here and wondered what they caught. Trout, presumably—and she had read somewhere that there were special seasons, so presumably April was in the trout season.

She was quite charmed with the idea; it was so new to her, so unexpected, to find herself in what amounted to a sort of small-scale palace full of fishermen. She smiled in delight at Travers and hugged his arm. "It's super, isn't it?"

"Not bad. Look, you go up to your room and settle in. I'll meet you in the cocktail lounge for a pre-dinner drink—shall we say about six-thirty?"

Nothing about Corinne's room caused her to change her opinion of the Burney House. She had her own bathroom and shower, her own TV set, even her own tea-maker arranged neatly on the bedside table with today's gourmet menu in a special folder lying on top of it.

She experienced a sense of relief. The episode on the moors had made her feel that the clothes she had packed would be useless, but certainly in this elegant and comfortable hotel thin shoes and lightweight dresses wouldn't be out of place. She unpacked, eyeing each item with pleasure as she slipped it on a hanger : soft checkered wool, little suits of sprigged print, shimmery sequins for evening, vivid jersey trouser suits . . . all high fashion and all relatively unworn. She had felt that, before she left London, she'd better stock up. As a result, she was pretty well broke—but what was money, after all !

She enjoyed the luxury of a hot bath into which she

tipped a good measure of her favourite bath essence. In her housecoat, she surveyed her wardrobe : what should she put on? Something to make an impact, but not over-stated. She chose at last a maxi-dress in navy glazed cotton with a demure white collar and a red ribbon bow at the throat. Above it her reddish-brown hair gleamed in happy contrast; she let it fall loose and full to her shoulders, went sparingly on make-up, and turned away from her mirror looking, she hoped, quietly sophisticated.

The cocktail lounge was rather full when she got downstairs, but Travers wasn't there. Instead, across the room, she caught sight of a familiar mop of ashen brown hair. Duncan Donaldson was seated at a table lit by a little rose-shaded lamp, and was listening with a smile to a girl opposite him.

Hesitating about whether to go in and wait, Corinne paused in the open doorway. The movement of the door had caused one or two heads to turn, Duncan's among them. He waved, and she raised a hand in reply, but made no move to go in. With a word to his companion Duncan got to his feet and came across to her.

"Well, Cinderella, so you got to the ball. Come away in and let me buy you a wee drappie."

"A what?"

"A drink. You'll have to learn the language if you want to stay in the district. Come along." He conducted her to his table. "May I introduce Miss Isabel Armstrong, a friend of mine. Isa, this is ... Corinne Something-or other—I'm afraid I never did learn the rest?"

"Corinne Lenwood. How do you do, Miss Armstrong?"

"Call me Isa, everybody does. Take a chair. What'll you have?"

She was a striking girl, older than Corinne by a couple of years and a little older yet in her manner and bearing; there was something forceful and keen about her that to Corinne's way of thinking would have been more expected in a town-dwelling career girl.

"You're here on holiday, Corinne?" she enquired.

"No, my firm's opening an office in Hawick."

"What firm is that?"

"Eldin Consultants. It's a London firm—this is a new venture, coming north."

"Think you're going to like it?"

"That's a leading question," Duncan put in. "So far she's only been here a few hours, but she's already been lost in a mist, trapped in a marsh, and baffled by the dialect."

"Don't mind him," Isa said. "He likes to look on the wry side of everything. Even if all these things really have happened, I think you'll find this isn't a bad place to live."

"You belong here, do you?"

"Born and bred. Armstrong's a Border name."

"A tribe of cattle thieves and brigands," Duncan said. "You'll notice Isa wears her hair cut short—that's a family tradition among the Armstrong women so that in a fight the enemy couldn't drag them away by the hair."

"Absolute nonsense!" Isa cried, laughing. She smoothed the soft cap of short brown hair. "Eighteen pounds this hair-do cost me, in the best salon in Edinburgh."

"Perhaps you'll give me the address?" Corinne said.

"In London I used to go to Vidal. It'll take me a while to find good dress shops and things."

"Oh, clothes are no problem—at least not for me. I move about quite a lot so I can always drop in somewhere in Glasgow or Edinburgh." Seeing Corinne's questioning look she added, "I'm a journalist. I work for the *Border Messenger*."

"That must be very interesting," Corinne murmured. Of course . . . that accounted for the sparkle and drive she generated.

"You're staying in the hotel?" Isa went on. "It's rather good, I think you'll find. Mrs. Patterson's a Cordon Bleu cook."

"I suppose we'll be here for a week or two," Corinne said, "until we find something else."

"We," Duncan echoed. "Meaning you and the man in the four-wheel drive. Was he a husband?" He touched her left hand. "No, I see he wasn't."

"He's my boss—Travers Eldin. His father owns the firm."

"Eldin Consultants, I think you said. What do they consult about? Law?"

"Can't be that, Duncan," objected Isa. "Scottish law is quite different from English."

"No, they're engineering consultants. Mr. Eldin feels there's a lot of opportunity north of the Border, and he's usually right."

"Could be, what with these development projects and so forth. There's more to be done at Cumbernauld, I hear."

"There's plenty to be done around here too, what with the motorway and everything."

"Motorway?" said Isa. "What motorway?"

"Oh, I'd have thought you'd know, being a journalist.

That's what Trav's come up for—to oversee the survey. I suppose that's why he chose this hotel, because it happens to be so handy for this particular stretch of the route."

There was an odd little silence.

"Where exactly is it going, this motorway?" Duncan enquired.

"It's to link up the A697 with the A7, I think."

"By way of the Burneybank?"

"Oh, they haven't quite decided yet. That's what Eldin Consultants have got to do—recommend the best route."

"To whom? The County Council?"

"No, no—the Ministry of Highways."

Isa finished her drink rather quickly and got up. "Excuse me," she said. "I've just remembered an important appointment."

"I bet you have," Duncan said, raising an ironic eyebrow. "So long, Isa—see you in the headlines." To Corinne he went on, "Does your firm do much work for the Ministry of Highways?"

"Yes, but Mr. Eldin senior usually handles it all himself. This is the first time Travers has ever been put in charge of a preliminary survey."

"And I fancy it will be the last."

"I beg your pardon?" Corinne was astonished. "What makes you say that?"

"Oh, just a hunch I have."

"I can't imagine what you mean! Travers is very good at his job."

"No doubt."

"And as you only met him for two minutes you couldn't possibly make any sort of judgement about him."

"You're quite right."

"Then what did you mean?"

He studied her in the subdued light of the little table lamp. "How long have you worked for him?' he asked.

"Not quite a year. Why?"

"You're very fond of him."

"I really don't know why you should jump to that conclusion," she said, going fiery red but thankful that the dim light made it less noticeable.

"I didn't have to jump. I was pushed to that conclusion by the way you rushed to his defence when you thought I was criticizing him. You *are* fond of him?"

"Well, yes. B-but even if I weren't," she stammered, "a secretary owes loyalty to her employer."

"Loyalty . . . yes." He spoke in a musing tone. "That's a necessary qualification in a secretary." He paused, then added, "Discretion too, wouldn't you say?"

"Discretion . . . ?" Something in the way he spoke the word made her stare at him. She felt a wave of apprehension. "Have I been indiscreet?"

He looked past her at the door. "Here comes your employer now," he murmured. "Why don't you ask him?"

He rose, gave her a little bow, and made his way to the exit. Corinne saw the two men exchange a nod as they passed. A moment later Travers was taking the chair Duncan had vacated.

"Sorry I'm a bit behind the time I suggested, darling," he remarked. "I've been on the line to Dad, telling him how things are going. You know what he's like once he gets started."

She knew only too well. Norman Eldin would have wanted the minutest details of all the work in progress.

But to judge by Trav's untroubled look, his father had been satisfied by what he had to report.

"You do look nice, Corinne," he went on, his eye roving over her.

"So do you," she replied. She felt they made an elegant couple, she in her Dior Boutique dress and Trav in his Hardy Amies suit and shirt.

The barman came for their order. She shook her head, indicating her still unfinished sherry, then said when they were alone again : "I was talking to a very interesting girl just before you came."

"Oh? I thought you were talking to that chap who swept you off your feet on the hill!"

She laughed, to cover a sense that Travers wasn't exactly pleased about that incident. "This girl was with him—a rather marvellous-looking girl, with big dark eyes in a broad-cheekboned face. Sort of Slavonic, almost."

"Slavonic? Here?"

"No, no, I only meant she *looked* it. She says she's a Borderer from way back. Works for the local paper."

"Mm . . ." Travers said, without interest. He sampled the potato crisps from the bowl on their table. "Are you hungry? I must admit I am, and the menu is great. They've got local-caught trout with almonds—we ought to sample it."

"Just as you like, Trav." She hesitated. "You don't mind my chatting with a journalist on the local paper?"

"Not a bit. Why should I? So long as you don't talk about the survey for the motorway, you have my permission to chat with whoever you like."

"But . . . but, Trav—I did!"

"What?"

"I chatted about the survey to Isabel Armstrong."

Travers leapt to his feet, at the precise moment that the barman was approaching with his drink. His shoulder hit the salver; the glass slid to one side, sending its contents all over the expensive suit. But he paid no attention to that. He was staring at Corinne in dismay.

"Corinne, how could you?"

She didn't know what to say. She met his angry gaze. "I'm—I'm sorry, Trav."

"How could you be so stupid?"

"I didn't know I wasn't supposed to . . ."

"Not supposed to? Surely your common sense should have told you it was highly confidential?"

"I'm sorry, Trav, I really am. Will it cause a lot of trouble?"

"Trouble? The Ministry officials will be furious. And my father will skin me alive." He waved aside the waiter, who was dabbing ineffectively at the spilt liquid. "I'll have to ring him straight away and tell him what's happened."

"Oh, dear . . ." She knew what an ordeal this would be. Norman Eldin wasn't a man to let anyone off lightly. She felt tears begin to prick behind her eyes, partly for herself but mostly for the misery she had brought upon Travers. "Let me ring him," she suggested in a shaking voice.

"You? You've done enough damage for one day," he riposted. And then, just before he turned on his heel and walked out: "I'll never forgive you, Corinne—never!"

CHAPTER TWO

THE next half-hour was the longest Corinne could ever remember. Travers took the call in his room, so Corinne sat on for a while in the bar. But the scene between them had caused some attention; she felt awkward and embarrassed. After about ten minutes she got up, without any clear idea where she was going. The idea of having dinner was unattractive—her appetite had completely gone. She went to her room, but to sit there in miserable suspense was unbearable.

Finally she snatched up a coat and went out. It was about eight o'clock of a cool, bright April evening; the sun was declining towards the hilltops, bathing the glens in deep shadow. She took a path from the hotel grounds that led gently up through some birch and pine until, unexpectedly, she came upon a clearing. A narrow footpath crossed it through the coarse grass; she followed it.

In the curve of the hill a castle stood, on guard over the valley. Perhaps it wasn't much of a castle compared with Windsor or the Tower of London, but it stood like a sentinel on its crag, sombre and lonely. Most of it was in ruins; only the circular tower was intact, rearing up like the barrel of some great cannon with its battlements black against a sky of orange and cinnamon cloud.

In Corinne's experience, castles were usually Ancient Monuments under the care of the Ministry of Works, with a green board telling the visitor how much he had to pay to get in. But this place was utterly deserted. There was no price-of-admission notice. A blackbird flew out of the empty doorway. Intrigued—even momentarily forgetting her troubles—she moved forward.

Inside the tower there were heaps of moss-covered stones, presumably the floors of the upper rooms which had fallen in. The light came in from overhead—the roof had gone. She saw a heavy stone staircase winding upwards in a spiral against the inner wall; the view from the battlements must be tremendous. She gathered her long skirt close against her legs and began to mount the stairs.

At the seventh step her head came level with a window slit. She looked out. She could see the copse of trees through which she had walked. Another five steps took her to another window, looking out on to a different aspect. Of course! These slits were for defence—as the enemy approached the archer posted here would loose his arrow, and so the windows gave different vantage points to make sure every point of attack was covered.

When she reached the next window she was halfway up the tower, a height of about twenty-five feet. The view this time was back towards the wood, but because she was higher she could see beyond it to the hotel. The westering sun flooded it with a golden light so that the windows sparkled and the lawns shone emerald green.

Beyond the main building there was another—a square, rather uncompromising building, although apparently as old as the hotel. What puzzled Corinne was that close to it there were some cubes and squares of red or yellow. She couldn't imagine what they could be; they were a little too much in the shadow of the building to be distinguishable.

She realized the shadows were growing rapidly longer. Soon it would be dark. She didn't much fancy walking back through the woods on her own in the dark. Besides, it was growing distinctly chilly.

Pulling her coat about her, she turned away from the arrow-slit. But now something strange had occurred: the inside of the tower was in almost complete darkness! She stopped, her breath catching in her throat. What had happened?

A moment's thought explained the change. The sun had sunk behind the hill so that the top of the tower was in its shadow—and since such light as got into the building came through the space at the top, the inside was now very dark.

Well, no use waiting. The longer she hesitated the darker it would grow. Picking up her skirts again in one hand, she used the other to feel her way down by the wall.

She had forgotten, though, that five or six steps down there was another arrow slit. When her hand encountered this she had a momentary panic—it felt as if the wall had disappeared. She lost her balance and fell, going over the side of the staircase into a terrifying blackness that rushed past her as she dropped twenty feet.

She hit the pile of ruined stones. All the breath was knocked out of her. Her senses went reeling. She was convinced she was going to faint.

But after a moment she discovered she was still completely conscious. Better still, so far as she could tell she was relatively unhurt. The moss and other vegetation growing among the stones had acted as a sort of quilt, to break her fall. She drew several deep breaths, moved her arms and legs experimentally to make sure nothing was broken, then began to get up.

Or attempted to. But, oddly enough, though there was nothing wrong with her, she couldn't get to her feet. She simply couldn't understand it. It was like a nightmare. She tried again, more vigorously. This time she moved about two inches from the horizontal position, but was immediately pulled back.

Panic seized her. She made a struggling effort. But though all her muscles responded she couldn't get to her feet.

And now the weight of her own body was pressing down on the vegetation on which she was lying. Little thorns and prickles penetrated the fine wool hopsack of her coat and the thin cotton of her dress, pressing into her skin.

That was when she understood what had happened. The plant growing among the stones was some kind of gorse or rose, and she was caught in the tangle—her coat and her long skirt and her hair were enmeshed among the thorns.

"No, no!" she sobbed, horrified at the thought. What had Duncan said earlier today about a sheep caught in the thickets—"it could stay there for a day and a night unless somebody sets it free . . ."

"Let me go!" she cried. "Let me go!" But it was no use; she needed to free her arms so as to be able to reach up and untangle her hair, before she could ever hope to get free.

The darkness all around her was now intense. She felt as if she was trapped at the bottom of a well.

"Help!" she shouted. "Help! Somebody!"

But nobody answered.

Staring up through the tower, she could see the stars shining brightly. It must be very late. Yet wait a moment—hadn't she heard that even in the daytime you can see the stars from the bottom of a well?

All at once she was overwhelmed by a sense of her own loneliness and helplessness. Tears welled up, and she began to cry.

Just as the first excess was over, she heard a voice.

"Who's there?"

"Help!" she called. "Help, help! I'm in here—in the tower!"

There came the sound of footsteps. The inside of the building was lit with a faint glow.

"Who's there? Who is it?"

"It's me—Corinne Lenwood. I'm caught by the thorns!"

"Good heavens!" The voice was unmistakable. "I thought you were Catherine herself!"

"That's Duncan Donaldson, isn't it? Please help me— I fell from the staircase and now I can't get up!"

He came into her line of vision. The light was from a heavy-duty torch he was carrying. "My dear girl! What a fix you're in! Are you hurt?"

"Only bruised, I think. But I'm all tangled up..."

"Just a minute, keep still. You're only making it worse." He played the light on her; since he was behind it she couldn't see him at all, but it suddenly came to her what a fool she must look, trapped like a kitten in a skein of wool. "Right," he said, "I see the solution. I'll untangle your hair and unfasten your coat. You should then be able to stand up, but you'll have to leave the coat among the twigs—it would take hours to separate it from the spines."

"Never mind about the coat. Please let's get out of here."

"Right-oh." He laid the torch on the ground so as to have both hands free. She felt him undo the two big buttons holding the coat. "Now you should be able to wriggle your arms out of the sleeves a bit—yes? Good. Keep still now. I'm going to get to work on your hair." He knelt beside her, his fingers gently taking the strands one at a time. "In different circumstances I could imagine enjoying this very much," he remarked. "Oh, hang it, as soon as I let go it falls back on another twig."

"Perhaps you'd better cut it, Duncan. Have you got a penknife?"

"Cut it?" he said, horrified. "And wreck this beautiful hair-do? Never!"

"Please don't tease," she said, her voice quavering. "I want to go *home*."

"I'm sorry. Just keep still, Corinne. I'll be as quick as I can." His voice had completely changed. "If I put my handkerchief . . . yes . . . that keeps the thorns away . . . good, just another second or two." He leaned back on his heels. "Now," he said, "I'm going to put my arms round your waist and pull—and you should be free."

He got to his feet, then leaned over her. She felt his arms go between her coat and her dress. "Ready?"

"Ready."

"One, two, three—up!"

Next moment she was on her feet and falling forward against him. Her hair had been pulled and tugged, and some rending sounds from her skirt told her that it was past praying for. But she was free.

"Thank you," she gasped, "oh, thank you."

"Now, now! Don't cry. What are you crying for?

You're all right. A few wisps of hair left behind on the bush, but otherwise as right as rain. As for the coat, if you give Andy Lennox a fivepence piece tomorrow, he'll be happy to come up here and disengage it for you. There, there..." He stroked her hair softly.

She leaned against him, shivering. Was it merely from reaction? She couldn't account for the inexplicable weakness that swept over her at his touch.

For some time they stood like this in the eerie light from the torch, circled around by thick walls of stone that isolated them not only from the world outside but from time itself. They might have been in some other galaxy, in some other era. For a breathless interval nothing else seemed to exist except their two selves.

And then something rustled in the undergrowth, and Corinne jumped with fright. "What's that?"

"Don't be afraid—it's probably only a mouse or a shrew. Come along, I'd better get you home."

"What were you doing out at this time of night anyway?" Corinne demanded as he helped her to the doorway.

"This time of night?" he repeated, amused. "It's only just on nine o'clock."

As they came out into the open she saw that this was true. Outside it was much lighter than in the tower, although daylight was gone. It was much colder.

"Just a minute," he said. He took off the windcheater he was wearing to drape it round her shoulders. "Is that better? We don't want you to catch a chill. Can you walk?"

"I'm fine, thanks. I ... I'm glad I don't have to go back through that wood alone."

"Why not? I often do."

"At night?"

"Yes, when I'm not botanizing."

"I didn't know anybody botanized in the dark."

"Oh, there's a lot we don't know about plants at night. You know moths and other insects fly about at night, so obviously they must pollinate flowers that attract them. You know tobacco flowers have a strong perfume at night."

"Have they? I didn't know."

"Well then, you've heard of night-scented stock? That's the kind of thing that I go to look at by torchlight."

It was a hobby that had never entered her ken before. She murmured something to that effect.

"You're not interested in ecology?"

"I ... er ... I'm not even sure what it is."

"It's the interdependence of everything in Nature. The more cities and towns get built up, the more it's important to understand what the effect will be. For instance, to build houses we have to give up farmland. Giving up farmland means fewer birds and insects. Fewer insects can mean that the fruit trees don't get pollinated. If apple trees aren't pollinated it could mean no apples for the people in those houses to eat."

"Good gracious! I'd no idea."

A silence fell between them. They came to the copse of pine and birch. Instinctively she shrank closer to Duncan. He put his arm round her shoulders. "Come on," he said, "it's only trees."

They walked on over the soft carpet of leaves and pine needles.

"Who's Catherine?" she asked suddenly.

"Who?"

"When you appeared on the scene a while ago—you said you thought I was Catherine."

34

"Aha! So you thought all this talk about the environment was only a blind, eh?"

"No, no," she replied, flustered, "and anyway it's none of my business."

"A very beautiful girl, Catherine.

> 'Like to the fawn, her step is light,
> And lovely is she to my sight,
> The bonny Lady Catherine.'

She died in the seventeenth century of a broken heart, waiting for her true love to come back from one of those ever-recurring Border feuds. She used to watch for him from the battlements up there—it's called Catherine's Tower."

"Oh, how sad!" Corinne exclaimed. "Poor girl."

"Oh, it was always happening in those days. Have you never heard any of the Border Ballads?"

"I don't believe I have . . ."

> " 'Lady Nancy she died as it might be today
> Lord Lovel he died on the morrow.
> Lady Nancy she died out of pure, pure grief,
> Lord Lovel he died out of sorrow.'

We take love seriously in the Borders, you see."

"Are you making fun of me again?" she enquired with suspicion.

"Perish the thought. I don't think you're in any position to have fun made of you. Did you by any chance tell Eldin about our conversation in the hotel?"

"Yes."

"And?"

"He was furious."

"I rather thought he might be," Duncan murmured.

"Especially as Isa will have it on the front page of the *Messenger* on Friday."

"Oh . . . she won't, will she?"

"If her editor thinks it's important—and I expect he will."

"It was all supposed to be confidential. But no one told me."

"But surely, as the papers passed through your hands, you must have seen they were marked 'Confidential'?"

"I've never seen any papers connected with the motorway. Mr. Eldin senior keeps things like that in his own hands. You must realize that Travers was only given control of this survey a few days before he left for Scotland, and he put the papers straight into his briefcase. *I* was busy winding up various things for him in London until today."

"I see."

"Of course I realize now I was too talkative," Corinne went on, impelled by an urge to justify herself, "but it never occurred to me the thing was a secret. I mean, you'd take it for granted that people would know that a six-lane highway was going to be cut through their district."

"You would indeed," he agreed bitterly.

They walked on in silence until they reached the gardens of the hotel. Corinne was overcome with reluctance to go through the hall with her hair in a mess and her skirt tattered. "I must look a sight," she faltered.

"Go you in the side door, then," suggested Duncan. "It's the one the fishers use when they come in wet and muddy. There's a staircase to the left—this way." He led her to a door which opened to his touch, to reveal a stone-floored room cluttered with damp gear and lit by a low-powered lamp. Even by this light she felt self conscious about her appearance and was turning away in confusion, but he prevented her. "You look like one of the raggle-taggle gypsies-o! It's rather effective."

"Oh . . . please . . . I must get tidied up . . ."

"Have you eaten yet tonight?"

"No, but I don't want to—"

"Nonsense, you must eat."

"No, really, I'm not hungry—"

"Look here, you've had a hard day and quite a few shocks. I'll get Mrs. Patterson to send you up something on a tray—"

"Oh, no, I should hate that!" The idea of sitting alone in her room, like a school child in disgrace (and of course she *was* in disgrace) was dismal.

"Should you?" He smiled, but whether in sympathy or in amusement at the dolefulness of her tone, she wasn't sure. "All right, then, go upstairs and make yourself less of a gypsy. I'll meet you in the dining-room in half an hour."

"But you don't want to bother—"

"Don't I? How can you tell?"

"Well, I mean, haven't I been enough nuisance for one day?"

He laughed. "I haven't had dinner yet. Either I go home and eat cold beef sandwiches alone, or I share Mrs. Patterson's excellent cooking with you. But if it's the latter, do be quick. I'm starving!"

He gave her a little push towards the interior of the hotel. Still a little puzzled that he should put himself out any further for her, Corinne obeyed the gesture.

Upstairs she showered quickly and, in place of the muted glamour of the ruined long dress, she put on a warm and comfortable trouser suit in violet-coloured wool. She was grateful that it hid the scratches and bruises on her arms and legs. About those on her face there was little to be done, but luckily her hair, once brushed into smoothness again, fell forward on her cheeks to conceal the worst.

Ahead of schedule she took the lift down to the hall. When she went into the dining-room Duncan rose to greet her. He too had changed, from his sweater and jeans to a very formal dark suit. It made him look quite different.

"How did you manage to get home to change, and back so quickly?" she asked in surprise.

"I practically live on the premises. What used to be the granary of the Burney House is now both my home and my place of business—"

"Oh, now I understand! Those yellow and red things I could see from the tower—they were tractors?"

"Quite right. They live downstairs. I live upstairs in what used to be the loft. You must come and have a look some time."

"I'd love to. Only ..."

"What?"

"I don't know whether I'll be here much longer."

The waitress came at that moment with the first course, a delicious fish soup. "I hope you don't mind," Duncan said. "I ordered for both of us so that it would be ready when you appeared."

"Of course I don't mind. This is delicious."

"I'm glad you like it—it's one of Mrs. Patterson's specialities." After a moment's pause he said, "What do you mean, you don't know whether you'll be here much longer?"

She sighed. "I should imagine I'll get the sack."

Though the smell of the spicy soup had made her

38

ravenous, her appetite deserted her again. She pushed away her plate.

"Eat your soup," Duncan urged. "It'll do you good."

"I couldn't—I'm sorry. I'm just not hungry."

He studied her for a moment. "It upsets you to think of leaving?"

"Well. . . naturally."

"You enjoy the job?"

"Oh, it's not the job! I can get another job in London. It's . . . it's . . ."

"Travers Eldin?"

Nodding, she looked down. "I only came north because of him."

"I see. And how does he feel?"

This was a question Corinne was quite incapable of answering. She knew that Travers had a great deal of feeling for her, but whether it matched her own she couldn't say.

"It won't rest with Trav anyway," she said. "His father will make the decision—he always does where business is concerned."

"Do I get the impression that Mr. Eldin is a bit of a tartar?"

She made no reply to this. Mr. Eldin was the head of the firm and loyalty forbade that she should say anything critical about him to a stranger. Not that Duncan was a stranger. It was odd how well she felt she knew him considering she'd only seen him for the first time that afternoon.

The waitress returned, and was scandalized to find Corinne's plate untouched. "What's wrang wi' the bisque?" she demanded in anxiety.

"Nothing, Nell, nothing. Miss Lenwood just doesn't feel like it."

"But a body must eat. Should I bring you ither thing, miss? For a first course?"

"No, thank you."

"We'll go on to the soufflé, Nell. Perhaps that will tempt her."

"I surely hope so, or Mistress Patterson will be gey stricken. Yourself must tell the young lady, sir, that the mistress takes a special care of the food and—"

"Yes, yes, Nell, I'm as keen to see our guest eat as you are. Away with you for the soufflé."

As Nell hurried away Corinne smiled and shrugged. "Since I'm not going to stay it doesn't matter, but I'm sure I'd never get the hang of the language. They have some strange expressions."

"I suppose so. 'Gey stricken' means 'rather upset'—"

"Yes, but she called you 'Yourself', almost as if you weren't there or something."

"Oh, it's just a term of respect. The doctor or the minister is often referred to as 'Himself'." He spoke dismissively because, it appeared, he had more important matters to discuss. "Where's your boss now?"

"Telephoning his father, I expect."

"Still? It was a couple of hours ago that you broke the bad news to him, surely?"

Corinne realized that this was so. She rather wondered why Travers hadn't sought her out—but then maybe he had done so while she was out getting embrangled with a thorn bush.

"It's no good thinking about it," she sighed. "The damage is done . . . although," and she looked perplexed, "I'm not sure *what* damage, really."

"Well, the *Messenger* will have at least a news item about the new road, maybe a headline. It could be very important for the area, you know. The two main industries are sheep-rearing and tweed—and the tweed mills may find the motorway a big asset. Of course a lot depends on how soon it's comng."

"I believe they're hoping to begin in eighteen months' time, if the survey is satisfactory."

"Satisfactory . . . I wonder what that means."

"The surveyors have to suggest the most economical route, that's to say if they have a choice between going along a valley, which is easy, or going over a mountain, which is difficult and expensive, they choose the valley. That sort of thing."

Nell came back bearing the soufflé. "Now I hope Yourself will see this isna wastit," she said severely, setting it down between them. "I'm awa' for the vegetables."

Corinne began to laugh. "Yourself had better behave yourself, or Nell will be after you!"

"She's a bit of a tyrant, isn't she? I've known her all my life, you know. She used to chase me out of her backyard when I was a boy and swung on her washline." He picked up the serving spoon. "But you are going to have some of this, aren't you? It's duck, and really very good, and what's more it'll slip down easily even if you aren't very hungry."

"And besides, Nell will be cross if you don't persuade me." But she accepted the helping together with the delicate green vegetables Nell had brought. It was indeed delicious : her hunger returned with the first mouthful.

"When I saw you up on the Burneybank this afternoon," Duncan resumed, "you were with Travers."

"Yes, he'd taken me to show me the survey team."

"So that means they're going along the Burney Glen."

"Well, they're *looking* at it."

41

"A six-lane highway?"

"Yes."

"There isn't room for a six-lane highway along the valley bottom."

"Oh, they'd excavate part of the hillside."

"Burneybank?" He looked shocked.

"Ye .. es."

"But the roses? The burnet roses? They'd be bull-dozed away!"

"I'm afraid so. Still, there are plenty more elsewhere, aren't there? You said it was one of the commonest roses in Scotland."

"I don't deny that," he said slowly, "but that hillside is a well-known spot—people climb the opposite slope to see the Burneybank in bloom."

"Oh. I didn't realize that . . ."

"All my life . . . and my father's life before me . . . they've always been there, the burnet roses. They were there in the days of Mary Stuart—what you would call Tudor times. They *can't* take away the burnet roses!"

Corinne was almost glad that at that moment Travers walked into the dining-room. He came directly to their table.

"They told me at the desk that you were here," he said, ignoring Duncan. "Come along, I want to talk to you, Corinne."

"Corinne would like to finish her meal, I think," Duncan interposed.

"If you don't mind, I'm speaking to my secretary," said Travers. "Come on, Corinne."

She half rose.

"Sit down," said Duncan. "Whatever your employer wants to say, it can wait ten minutes."

"No, really, I—"

"I'll thank you not to interfere," Travers said simultaneously, speaking to Duncan. "It doesn't concern you."

"I rather think it does, if it's anything to do with the motorway through the Burney Glen."

"Corinne, what have you been saying?"

"Nothing! At least, I—"

"Didn't I tell you not three hours ago that the Caithdale Motorway project was highly confidential?"

"Highly confidential to whom?" Duncan said, getting to his feet. "Not to the people who live in Caithdale, obviously! We're the last to hear of it. I certainly feel I owe a debt of gratitude to Corinne—"

"Oh, you do, do you? You haven't any scruples about leading her on to talk about it—"

"In a thing like this it looks as if I can't afford scruples—"

"Duncan!" Corinne gasped, horrified.

"I'm sorry, Corinne, but it's a fact. If there's no other way of getting information—"

"You mean it was all a trick? All the concern over my troubles and coaxing me to stay and eat—you were just *using* me?"

He coloured. "Perhaps no one ever acts without mixed motives—"

"Oh, how despicable!" She jumped up, turning to Travers. "Come along, Trav, I'm ready to talk to you whenever you want."

She brushed past Duncan Donaldson, who made no attempt to stop her. She took Trav's arm and went with him to the coffee lounge, almost eager to hear whatever bad news he had to report in her urgency to get away.

At the door she passed Nell, who was gasping in

dismay. "Yon's no way to speak to Himself!" she protested. "You should be ashamed!"

"He's the one that should be ashamed," Corinne replied with a stifled sob in her voice.

"For heaven's sake," muttered Travers, "do we have to bring the servants into it? Come and sit down and talk sense!"

The lounge was almost deserted since most of the other guests were anglers who had gone early to bed ready for an early start on the river next morning. Collecting herself, Corinne said, "Did you get through to your father?"

Trav nodded. His grim expression showed how unpleasant it had been.

"He was wild. We had a discussion and then he said he'd better contact a few people and ring back. So I had to stand by the phone for over an hour until he came through again."

"What did he say?"

"He's catching the night train. He'll be here in the morning. And Corinne—" he gave her a stricken glance —"he wants to talk to *you*."

CHAPTER THREE

CORINNE went to bed with the expectation of staying awake all night. But, as Duncan had remarked earlier, she had had a hard day. So after tossing and turning for a few minutes she fell asleep suddenly, like going over a precipice, and if she had troubled dreams she couldn't remember any of them next morning. It was by no means early when she woke, and she didn't hurry about dressing because she suffered some slight stiffness after her fall. She went downstairs at last about nine-thirty, heading for the dining-room rather in the spirit of "The condemned man ate a hearty breakfast".

Isa Armstrong was lingering in the hall. "Hi there, good morning!" she said with cheerful affability. "Mind if I join you?"

"Would it make any difference if I said no?"

"None at all." She followed Corinne to a table by the window, adding "Just coffee" to Corinne's order of eggs and toast. "Are you annoyed with me?" she enquired.

"I'm not exactly pleased."

"Himself said you went off in a great dramatic hoo-ha last night. Look, my bonnie wee lass, news is my business. I didn't *ask* you for the information you gave me, and I haven't made any improper use of it."

"N . . . no," Corinne agreed.

"In fact I haven't made *any* use of it so far. I filed the item with my editor and so far he's done nothing with it. He says it needs more 'body'."

"Which is why you're here."

"Ouch," said Isa. "You pack quite a punch, don't you?"

"You aren't here just for the pleasure of drinking coffee with me, I feel sure."

"Oh, now listen, Corinne—"

"Just ask your questions. If I can answer them, I will." Her breakfast was brought, and for a moment Corinne busied herself with buttering toast and pouring tea. As she did so she let her glance travel to the view beyond the hotel balustrade. The hills were emerald green under a quiet morning light, while on the leaves

45

of the trees the dew still sparkled. She would have loved to be out there in that peaceful world instead of in this doom-laden lull indoors awaiting Norman Eldin.

As she gazed she heard the thudding of hooves. A group of riders came along the soft verge of the road at a trot, and then one of them detached himself to swing off to the left as the others rode on through the village. He disappeared behind the greenery in the hotel gardens.

"Really, doesn't that man ever do any work?" Corinne said crossly. "He was out on the hills yesterday afternoon and here he is this morning riding with friends. When does he sell any tractors?"

Isa leaned forward to see what Corinne had been watching, but the riders had gone. "If it was Duncan, you can be sure he's always there when he's needed. Nobody buys a tractor on the spur of the moment, my dear—they chat about it at horse shows and agricultural fairs, and ring up for discussions. Then finally they take the plunge, but not before giving plenty of warning! As for going out riding—that's part of the way of life here. The Borders is horseman's country. Have you ever seen a Common Riding?"

"I don't even know what it is, I'm afraid."

"It's an old tradition, going back to the days when no community was safe. Each year the young men of a town will ride round the bounds of their district. That sounds a bit tame—but there's a pageant and a festival and dancing and competitions. As many as three hundred horsemen will take part in the events. Here at Burney it's called the Ride-out. Perhaps you'll see it."

"I rather doubt it."

"Did you get the push last night?"

"No, I didn't."

"You didn't? I *am* surprised. Duncan said—"

"Duncan keeps you well informed!"

"Of course he does. He'd do anything for me."

"Including collect information for you?"

"If he sees a good chance."

Corinne decided to give her attention to her breakfast instead of bothering any more about Duncan Donaldson and his friends. She expected to leave the village of Burney before the end of the day and never to see it or its inhabitants again.

"How far has your boss's firm got with its survey?" Isa asked.

"I'm sorry, I can't answer that."

"Have they made any recommendations about the direction of the motorway?"

"I don't know."

"What was Mr. Eldin's reaction when he heard you'd told me?"

"You know that already."

"Well, I heard he was hot and bothered. What did he do?"

"Didn't you hear that too? I'd have thought Mr. Donaldson would have told you."

"He did mention something about a phone call."

"Oh, really!" Corinne burst out. "He seems to get to know all that's going on!"

"Not quite everything, unfortunately. What was the result of the phone call?"

"I haven't the slightest intention of telling you."

But the result of the phone call made its appearance at that moment, in the shape of a bronze Citroën turning into the drive. This was Travers' car; he had set off earlier to meet his father off the night train at Berwick upon Tweed.

47

Despite herself Corinne stiffened at the sight. Isa, noting her anxiety, said: "Who is that? Who's in the car with Eldin?"

Since Isa could easily find out once Mr. Eldin registered at the hotel Corinne saw no point in concealment. "It's Mr. Eldin's father."

"The head of the firm? That must mean that he's worried."

And it also means my head is about to roll, Corinne said to herself.

"So what's he worried *about*?"

"I've no idea."

"Oh, come on, you must know."

"Even if I did, I shouldn't tell you."

"Why not?" Isa demanded in surprise. "After all, it's quite clear you've blotted your copy-book and you're for the high jump. So you don't owe any loyalty to the firm any more, do you?"

Turning her coat as quickly as that was an idea which struck Corinne as very distasteful. She busied herself with her tea-cup. Isa, seeing there was no more to be got out of her, gave her a rather patronizing pat on the hand and hurried out just in time to intercept Norman Eldin in the hall. Corinne preferred not to think how annoyed Mr. Eldin would be. It certainly wouldn't sweeten his temper for the forthcoming interview with herself.

Somehow she had expected to be summoned to the presence immediately. But time went by and nothing happened. When she had finished breakfast she sat on for a while. Then she went to the desk to ask if a message had been left for her. The answer was in the negative. At about eleven o'clock, greatly daring, she asked the receptionist to put her through by phone to Travers.

He was in his father's room, and not very pleased at being interrupted. "I can't talk now. We're busy."

"I just wondered if you could say when your father would want to see me, Trav. The suspense is killing me!"

"Oh, not till the afternoon, I think. We're going to Hawick to see a few people."

She couldn't help feeling it was rather heartless not to have told her this an hour ago.

"What ought I to do, then, Trav?"

"Good heavens, what does it matter! Please yourself."

He hung up. Hurt, Corinne did likewise.

Her first impulse was to pack up and go. She ran up to her room, took her suitcase from the wardrobe, and began whipping clothes off the hangers. She had got about four items folded when there was a tap on her door.

It was Travers. He stepped into the room and took her in his arms. "Darling, I'm sorry! I didn't mean to speak to you like that! Forgive me?"

She was surprised and delighted. All her hurt feelings vanished as his lips touched hers. It was so wonderful to have him rush to her like this, anxious to apologize and to make amends.

"You know how Dad affects me," he murmured, his brown eyes rueful. "He gets me so worked up I don't know what I'm saying. You do forgive me, sweetheart, don't you?"

"Of course I do. In fact I'm the one who should be apologizing, for landing you in all this trouble. Trav, if I could only undo what I've done—!"

"There's no hope of that, I'm afraid."

"Is your father *very* angry?"

"Not so much as I expected. I think his first outburst probably got most of it off his chest. Now his chief concern is to see how much damage has been done by the revelation, and what the reaction is from the local bigwigs. He's been on the telephone making appointments and so on. Later today we'll have a better idea."

"Wouldn't it just be better, Trav, if I took the train home right now?"

"No, don't do that. He wants to talk to you about that woman reporter."

"He met her as he came in, didn't he? She dashed out of the dining-room——"

"Yes, and she asked a few leading questions which he avoided. The point is, Corinne, she could actually be a help to us. That's why he wants to discuss her."

"I really don't know anything about her..."

"She's around somewhere—could you chat her up a bit?"

"Oh, Trav..."

"Do it for *me*, darling. It'd be such a help to know which way the local press is going to handle it."

Unwillingly she nodded.

"I must go, Corinne. I popped out to see you on the pretext of getting some papers from my own room— Dad will wonder where I've got to." He dropped a kiss on the top of her head and was gone.

She had seen Isabel Armstrong walking down towards the village. She picked up a blazer coat and went out to find her. Isa was in conversation with a group outside the post office, notebook at the ready. The conversation was in Lallands, so Corinne couldn't understand a word, but after some minutes Isa drew her interview to a close and came to join her.

"Were you asking them if they want a motorway? What did they say?"

"A fairly mixed reaction. I wish I could get a lead."

"How do you set about doing that?" Corinne enquired.

"I go out and about, finding out what people feel. In fact that's what I'm going to do now." She studied Corinne, and Corinne knew she was thinking there was a lot to be learned from her about Eldin Consultants. "Like to come with me?" she invited.

"I'd like to, very much," Corinne replied, hiding a smile. What an ironic situation! Isa was latching on to Corinne for what she could get out of her, and Corinne was doing exactly the same.

They got into Isa's little Morris Minor. Corinne thought her driving left a lot to be desired, but on these minor roads, deserted of traffic, it took them into no difficulties. She drew up at a little hump-backed bridge over a stream.

"This is the Caith Water. Gives the district its name —Caithdale. It's a famous trout stream, which is why..." She led the way down a steep and slippery track to the bank, where a solitary angler was casting a fly. He reeled in as they approached, looking a trifle disgruntled.

"Sorry to disturb, Colonel. Are they rising?"

"They certainly won't if you come roaring up in that tin can of yours and tramp about in commando boots." Nevertheless he raised his battered hat politely, glancing at Corinne with inquiry.

"This is Corinne Lenwood, who works for Eldin Consultants—"

51

"Ah, those villains! I've heard all about it! They needn't think they can come blundering down Caithdale laying everything flat for their juggernaut lorries! I'll take out a shotgun to them—"

"Now, now, Colonel," Isa soothed, "the scheme is only at the exploratory stage so far. No decision's been reached."

"The idea should never have been put up! This is one of the best stretches of fishing in the country. What d'you think it'll do to the fish if they start laying asphalt and diverting the stream?"

"Is that being suggested?" Isa said, looking surprised.

"Well, I had a crack with the laird on the phone, and so far as he's been able to work it out on the map, using guesswork and a certain amount of local observation, the motorway looks like coming in from the east by Nimo..." Here followed a great deal of geography that Corinne wasn't able to follow because she didn't know the district. The Colonel ended with ire, "They'll be spoiling some of the best fishing, some of the best views, and some of the best farmland in the Borders. I won't let them do it, I simply won't!"

Isa made sympathetic sounds. They left him whipping his rod over the gurgling waters, his face angry and anxious.

"Poor old chap. Colonel Walker retired here about ten years ago, for the sake of the fishing. It'll break his heart if anything happens to it."

"Still, a few fish aren't important—"

"Are they not!" Isa exclaimed. "Fishing is big business in the Borders. The owners of the fishing rights can 'let' a stretch of water for hundreds of pounds, and then there's the catch itself—trout and salmon, for hotels and shops. Show some sense, pet! The anglers will make a solid opposition to any motorway scheme if it harms the fishing."

Corinne hadn't thought of that. "It's so complicated!" she sighed. As they got back into the car she added, "Where now?"

"Let's go and talk to a few farmers. Some of them may be quite happy at the idea of a motorway if it means getting produce to market more easily."

Off they went, down a narrow lane that was scarcely more than a track. There were no houses to be seen, so that it came as a surprise when, rounding a bend, they saw a group of people in a field.

"Hello, what's going on?" Isa pulled up without warning, jerking them in their seats. She got out in haste, going to lean on the stone dyke. "Oh, I see! They're dowsing."

"Dowsing?"

"Water-divining."

Corinne leaned on the sun-warmed stones to watch. A very little and frail old lady, in a smart black coat and hat, was walking slowly towards them holding a forked twig in her hands. Her eyes appeared to be half-closed. The stem of the twig moved a little as she progressed over the grassy surface, but whether because of her own motion over the uneven turf or for some more mystic reason, Corinne couldn't tell.

"Do they actually believe in that nonsense?" she enquired.

Isa frowned. "It isn't nonsense. Believe me, it works. These people don't waste time on nonsense—they've got too much else to do."

"You mean that old lady has actually found water?"

"Water and other things besides. She's a Faa."

"A what?" Corinne said. It seemed to her she was

continually having to ask for explanations since she came to Burney—so many things were new to her. "What's a Faa?"

"It isn't a what, it's a who," said Isa. "The Faas were a clan of Border gypsies, very influential hereabouts for generations. No, really, I mean it. Look in the history books for this area, and you'll find them mentioned. They wandered about among the fighting families—the Lennoxes, the Ainslies, the Hardies, my own bunch the Armstrongs—and they were very useful because they could carry messages or sell information. They also had the sight."

"Second sight, you mean?"

"Of course. And Mrs. Moffat has it. She was a Faa before her marriage. She's been a dowser for about seventy years."

"I shouldn't have thought they needed to dowse for water," Corinne remarked. "There are brooks and streams everywhere."

"But not always on the surface. Just the point, you see—there could be an underground river just where you're thinking of building your house, so you call in old Mrs. Moffat to make sure the ground's solid and reliable."

"Is that what's happening now?"

"I'll find out." Isa went to a gate in the dyke, waiting for Corinne to follow her so that they could join the group. Once among them, she made inquiries in a low tone; everyone was subdued and respectful while the old lady moved gradually back and forth.

"In this case she actually is looking for water. Mr. Hamilton wants to put cattle in this pasture, so it means either bringing piped water to their drinking trough or finding a spring nearby."

There was an expectant "A-ah" from the onlookers. Mrs. Moffat's twig had jerked downwards significantly. She paused.

"Twelve feet doon," she announced, "in sandstane— you'll get it easy, Maister Hamilton."

The owner of the farm smiled with delight. "Ach, ye're a grand soul, Meg! Ye've saved me a mint o' money."

The old lady inclined her head in acknowledgement. She had an extraordinary regal bearing, with fine bones and snapping black eyes. Her hair was almost completely jet black except for one or two single silver threads glinting in the snail-shell coil at the nape of her neck.

Her glance lighted on Corinne. She moved towards her, almost like royalty at a garden party. "You're the girl from the motorway firm," she said.

Corinne stared. Was it witchcraft?

"Don't be alarmed," Mrs. Moffat said. "You're a stranger, and besides I've heard all about your pretty fox-coloured hair and your fine pale complexion—so you couldna be anyone else. You're a pretty child, my dear. Come and talk to me."

She took Corinne's arm—partly for support, Corinne felt, for she really was very old and the ground was uneven to her small feet in their neat little astrakhan-trimmed boots. Isa tacked herself on at the other side. The rest of the gathering trailed along behind them. Corinne was about to enquire where they were headed when all at once a farm truck came into view, parked in a corner of the next field. Mrs. Moffat and the farmer got into the front, everybody else clambered in the back, and they jolted off across the ploughed surface for some five minutes until they reached the farm. Here several people said goodbye and drove off in their own transport, but Mrs. Moffat was shown indoors respectfully.

She settled herself on a sofa in the comfortable living-room. "Come and sit down," she commanded, patting the place beside her.

Corinne obeyed.

"You've brought great trouble to us, Miss Lenwood."

"Oh, please, you mustn't blame *me*—"

"There will be great argument and unrest over this motorway. You must tell your employer that we don't want it."

"Why not, Mrs. Moffat?" Isa put in. "It could do a lot of good."

"I'm thinking the same thing," their host remarked. "I'm not just so sure it's a bad thing, Meg."

"Arthur Hamilton, you were always one to think of money first and true profit after. What good will it do us to have a road to take the wool to the mills faster, if there are no sheep from which to get the wool?"

"Och, there'll be sheep, Mistress Moffat. There have aye been sheep in Caithdale."

His wife gave a murmur of agreement, but the old lady shook her head. "Have you heard about the amount of land the highway will swallow up? And the levelling of the hillsides? Himself and Colonel Walker traced it out on a map. This I tell you, Maister Johnson —*my* farm will be cut in two, and what's left of it afterwards will be enough for a school playground, mebbe." She turned to Corinne. "Will you tell that to your employer?"

"I will," Corinne said, "but you must understand that he doesn't choose or make decisions."

"Does he not? I thought Himself said the surveyor chose the best route."

"Oh, yes, he recommends it to the Ministry. But the Ministry decides."

"Come, come," said Mrs. Hamilton, "your dinner is on the table now. Leave all this worrying talk and sit down to your meal."

Corinne and Isa were about to take their leave, but were hospitably pressed to stay. "There's plenty for all," the farmer's wife insisted. So they sat down in the big stone-floored kitchen to thick broth and home-made bread, chicken and salad, and a fruit pudding. Corinne couldn't eat all that was put before her. After the meal, tea was served, rather to the surprise of Corinne who was expecting coffee.

"Will you look in the tea-leaves for us?" Mrs. Hamilton ventured, looking hopefully at Mrs Moffat.

"Na, na, Alice—you know I don't go in for such foolishness. Tea-leaves and crystal balls have nothing to do with what's to be seen in the future or the past."

"But can you foresee anything for me?" she persisted.

"I can predict that you'll put on weight if you eat as much at every meal as you did at the last."

"Oh, *Meg*!"

The old lady watched Corinne set down her tea-cup. Then she reached across—not, however, to take the cup but, to Corinne's surprise, to take her hand. She felt the two wrinkled old palms cradle it, turning it a little from side to side. But Mrs. Moffat made no attempt to look at it, or to examine the lines.

"Love is a troublesome thing, child," she said gently. "And so is loyalty. Don't grieve too much if one runs counter to the other for a time."

Corinne was too taken aback to say anything. Isa said shrewdly: "Which should she place first, Mrs. Moffat?"

"Ah," said Mrs. Moffat, "Isa, Isa, you always want to use everything to your own advantage! Little you care if the girl is unhappy—all that concerns you is whether you get something out of her for your paper."

Isa sprang up. "That's not very kind—"

"The truth is often cruel. That's why you should never ask answers from the likes of me, if you can't bear honesty." Her voice was crisp and quiet; it conveyed absolute authority.

Arthur Hamilton said jovially, to lighten the atmosphere: "And what about my crops this year, Meg? Shall I have a good harvest?"

"Aye, aye, the oats will grow and the cabbage will thrive. But little you'll notice it when voices are raised and the stones are flying."

"Stones flying? Are you predicting a riot, Mrs. Moffat?" Isa said, almost with eagerness. "What a story!"

"Oh, de'il-may-care for that!" cried Mrs. Hamilton, quite depressed. "Don't look any further forrard, Meg! You're spoiling the luck of finding the water for us. Come now, have another cup of tea and we'll talk of better things."

"No, thank you, mistress, I must get back to my own concerns. Success to the house and those in it." She rose with some slight difficulty, accepting Corinne's help. As they went to the door together she murmured, "Don't trust that one too far, my dear. I see trouble in her shadow for you."

"I'm not expecting to be here after today, Mrs. Moffat," Corinne replied, "so you see it doesn't really—"

The descendant from the gypsy clan turned black, sharp eyes upon her.

"Next time you see me," she remarked, "I'll remind you of what you've just said. And remember my reply —it'll be many a long day before you leave this land Goodbye for the present, child."

She allowed herself to be helped into her car, a stately Wolseley at least twenty years old. Half hidden by the steering wheel, she raised a hand in farewell and drove off.

"Did she say she had a farm?" Corinne said wonderingly. "At her age?"

"She's one of the best sheep-farmers in the district, wins prizes at shows," Arthur Hamilton replied. "Ach, she's a wonder! Eighty-two if she's a day." He looked with respect at Corinne. "She took a real fancy to you, Miss Lenwood. You being a stranger, you dinna ken how lucky you are. She disna tak' to many."

"True, very true," said his wife. "One or two there are that she feels drawn to. Himself is one. Then there's the shepherd's wife over at Bellmuir. And now Miss Lenwood."

When she and Isa were back in the Morris, Corinne said in some perplexity, "When they say 'Himself' in the course of conversation, which 'Himself' do they mean?"

"Well, it depends on the subject. If they said 'the church steeple's falling down but Himself is doing nothing about it', they'd mean the minister."

"So which 'Himself' is it that Mrs. Moffat is fond of?"

"Oh, that's Duncan."

"Duncan?" Corinne felt she would never understand all the nuances of Border speech. As if it weren't enough that they spoke two languages, their own Border dialect and formal English, they had this special way of using words that quite defeated translation. "Maister Hamilton" meant something subtly different from "Mister Hamilton"; "Mr." Hamilton meant that you were a male surnamed Hamilton, but "Maister" gave you status, implied respect. And the old lady had addressed the farmer's wife as "Mistress". Corinne found it charming.

"Did you say Mrs. Moffat found other things besides water?"

"If she asked to. Some archaeologists called her in a couple of years ago and she found a Roman guardhouse for them."

"Here? So far north?"

"Of course. Hadrian's Wall is only a few miles away. Another time she found a burial site with swords and things—I think that was Saxon. She wasn't looking for it, she was dowsing for the Catherine Tower tunnel."

"Oh, I've seen the Catherine Tower," Corinne said, touching the faint scratches on her cheek. "I didn't know there was a tunnel."

"Nor there is—it's all fallen in. It used to go to the caves down by Caith Water." Isa glanced at her and grimaced with amusement. "I bet you find it hard to accept! Dowsing and second sight and secret tunnels!"

"It certainly isn't like London," Corinne agreed. "What was the tunnel for?"

"If you've seen the tower you'll know it used to guard the valley. The men on watch could go along the tunnel if they were besieged and get supplies from the caves by the river—such supplies, I may say, usually consisting of cattle and grain stolen from rival clans! Old Mrs. Moffat was asked to find the tunnel by the folk who bought the Burney House for a hotel—they thought it would make a tourist attraction because the

Catherine Tower is on their land. But the old girl said it was no use." Isa slowed to let a flock of sheep cross the road. "The caves are still there, of course. They go in from the banks of the Caith Water, not far from the spot where Colonel Walker was fishing."

"It certainly *isn't* like London," Corinne said.

For another hour or so Isa drove around, stopping to speak to people at random. Quite a few she knew by name, and Corinne realized that this was a close-knit community, quick to contact each other for discussion and advice. She began to feel less resentful towards Duncan for wanting to get information out of her : he probably felt he owed a duty towards his fellow countrymen. She tried to put herself in his position. If *she* belonged to a place like this and someone happened along babbling about motorways and bulldozers, wouldn't *she* feel obliged to take the opportunity of garnering facts?

After all, she was a stranger, a newcomer. Duncan had no obligations towards her.

Somehow that thought depressed her. By the time Isa delivered her back at the Burney House for tea, her spirits could scarcely have been lower.

Travers was standing at the window as she got out of the car. He waved and disappeared, to be waiting for her at the door of the lounge as she came into the hall.

"Darling, great news !" he burst out. "You're staying on !"

She drew up short to stare at him. Mrs. Moffat's prediction sounded again in her ears : "It'll be many a long day before you leave this land." How strange that she should have said that when Corinne had been absolutely certain she would be London-bound next day !

"How wonderful," she breathed. "You mean your father's forgiven me?"

"More or less. He's waiting in there—" he nodded towards the lounge. "We ordered tea to be brought as soon as you showed up."

"What ought I to do, Trav? Apologize at once, or what?"

"I'm not sure. I don't know all the ins and outs of it, but it seems it wasn't such a bad thing for the local people to get to know about the project. Somebody said to Dad that Lord Caithdale felt you'd performed a public service so shouldn't be victimized."

"Who's Lord Caithdale?"

"Goodness knows, some local bigwig. Anyway, darling, you don't have to leave and I don't have to do without you—isn't it marvellous?"

He held out his arms and she threw herself into them, to be hugged and kissed in congratulation.

It was unfortunate that Duncan Donaldson should choose that moment to come through the hotel entrance. As they drew apart he gave a cold little nod of greeting and walked on towards the dining-room.

Unaccountably, Corinne felt her elation ebb away.

CHAPTER FOUR

NORMAN ELDIN wasn't prepared to let her off without verbal punishment. "I don't have to tell you, Corinne, that this could easily have been disastrous. The Ministry of Highways only gives commissions to firms that it can trust, so the kind of disloyalty you displayed—"

"I wasn't disloyal, Mr. Eldin. I simply didn't *know* that the work was still under wraps—"

"Please allow me to finish," Mr. Eldin said, holding up a hand in remonstrance. He was a very handsome man, uncannily like his son except that his hair was iron grey and he sported a military moustache, a relic of his army days. "Giving information about our survey was wrong and, if it wasn't disloyal, it was certainly thoughtless. You accept *that*, I presume?"

"Yes, Mr. Eldin."

"However, it sometimes happens that a government department will allow a 'leak' of information to reporters. Luckily for you, this was about to happen quite soon with the Caithdale motorway. There had already been such trouble over the Galashiels Development Plan that it was felt they daren't have a repetition over this motorway."

"What happened over the Galashiels Development Plan?" she asked rather timidly.

"The local people stopped it dead. They just wouldn't have it. Of course they're entitled to choose woods and lakes rather than new housing and industry—that's their own affair, however mistaken I may think them. But the motorway is an absolute must and the only matter of discussion is the route it will take. The Ministry of Highways was not displeased to have the discussion opened. So, in fact, no harm's been done."

"I'm so glad."

"That doesn't alter the fact that you behaved with great carelessness and naïveté, Corinne. In the normal run of affairs I'd send you packing. But Travers here is inclined to think you'd be difficult to replace, which may be true. And from now on, naturally, we'll have to tread very carefully, which I think perhaps you've learned to do."

"Yes, Mr. Eldin."

"In any case, I've had a hint that it would look like 'victimization' if I sacked you, and I certainly don't want to start off on the wrong foot."

"No, Mr. Eldin."

"So let's regard the whole matter as closed. Ah, here's the tea. Will you pour, my dear?"

The last thing Corinne had expected from this interview was to be addressed as 'my dear' by Norman Eldin. It was not that he lacked warmth: he could be very affectionate towards his son at times, particularly when Travers had done something in exactly the way his father had advised and within the specified time schedule. But Norman Eldin was the kind of man who couldn't quite believe that "staff"—people he hired— were made of quite the same stuff as himself.

Corinne was sure that Mr. Eldin knew of the feeling she and Travers had for each other. She was equally sure he wasn't worried by it. He didn't mind his son having a friendship, or something more, with his secretary, so long as it didn't grow serious. She was convinced it had never crossed Mr. Eldin's mind that his son might actually want to marry Corinne.

The days that followed were extremely busy. Mr. Eldin decided to stay on for a while, to guide this new branch of the firm through this rather stormy launching period. He it was who selected the new office premises in Hawick, who arranged for their redecoration and the installation of telephones.

At first there was a great deal of talk about finding living quarters in Hawick. But the Burney House was such a very comfortable hotel that he decided to remain there: "After all, it's only for a couple of months at most!" The drive to the town, on uncrowded roads, was negligible compared with getting into London from Kent. Since he was staying on at the Burney House, there was no question but that Travers must stay too.

But Mr. Eldin rather balked at paying first-class hotel rates for a mere secretary. "I take it you'll be making more permanent arrangements as soon as you can?" he remarked to Corinne.

"Oh, yes, sir—as soon as I get time." It wasn't exactly easy. There was a lot of work at the office, which only left the weekends free—Saturdays, in fact, for the Scots insisted on observing Sunday as a day of rest, even when it came to showing a prospective client round a flat.

She asked the receptionist at the Burney House if she knew of anywhere. Amy, a pleasant young married woman, promised she would keep an eye open.

Two evenings later she was dining alone in the hotel. Travers and his father were at some civic function in Coldstream. Isabel Armstrong came in and, without invitation, sat down beside her. "I hear you're looking for digs?"

"Yes, I am."

"What about coming to share my pad? I've got a whole wing of an old house near Denholm, a few miles outside Hawick."

Corinne was startled. Hospitable though the Borderers were, she hadn't expected an offer like this, particularly from Isa, whom she wasn't sure she liked.

"Oh . . . it's very kind of you, but . . ."

"But what?"

"I haven't a car. How could I get back and forth to my job?"

"The local bus practically passes my door."

"Oh. That would be very convenient, of course, but . . ."

"But *what*?"

Corinne said bluntly: "Do you think it would be a good idea? After all, you're a journalist—you're on the lookout for news items and I'm in the middle of a tricky situation. If I said something I oughtn't to, would I have your word you wouldn't print it?"

Isa laughed with some annoyance. "That's asking a bit much."

"I suppose it is. But I couldn't feel easy otherwise."

"All right," said the other girl after a momentary hesitation, "suppose I gave you my word?"

Corinne's impulse was to respond: "Could I trust you to keep it?" And the answer to that, she knew instinctively, was "No". She remembered how Mrs. Moffat had said: "You always want to use everything to your own advantage," and she felt that the old lady spoke from a sure knowledge of her character.

The situation was hideously embarrassing. She coloured painfully. "Perhaps I could come and look at it?" she suggested. "If I don't find anything in the meantime."

"Fine. When can you come—tomorrow evening?"

"I'll be working late tomorrow," she replied, making a mental note to make sure that came true.

"Wednesday, then?"

"Thank you, I could manage that." That would give her the whole of tomorrow and most of Wednesday to find some alternative; then, if all else failed, she could say she didn't like Isa's flat.

"Come and have a drink on the strength of it."

"Oh . . . thank you, I'd rather not. I generally have coffee. You go ahead, though."

"Come along, we'll have coffee together in the lounge."

There was no escape without being downright rude. Inwardly annoyed with herself for allowing the situation to develop, she picked up her bag, folded the crossword puzzle she had been doing, and went with the other girl.

As they went in they saw Duncan sitting with friends at the far side. He waved a greeting.

"Fishing talk," Isa remarked as they turned to find seats for themselves. "That's one of the groups of anglers who are preparing a protest about the motorway." She looked keenly at Corinne as she said it.

Corinne had heard talk between Travers and the survey team about alterations to the flow of the Caith Water. She knew better than to breathe a word of it to her companion. The *Border Messenger* had come out with a couple of very fair reports about local reaction, but it was quite clear that the editor was waiting for something dramatic, some good cause for which he could campaign. The damage to the angling community might be just what he needed to use as a banner.

"Colonel Walker has done an opinion poll," Isa continued. "There isn't a single person connected with fishing who wants the motorway—not the anglers themselves, not the landlords who own the river banks, not the innkeepers where the anglers stay, not the merchants who buy the catch."

"I can't blame them."

"Why do you say that? Is the motorway going to mean diverting the river?"

Had she in any way implied that by her remark? Corinne tried to hear again in her mind the tone in which she had spoken; had there been any undertone of "I can't blame them for that in view of the blow that's going to fall"?

"I don't know anything about the route of the motorway," she said.

"What you really mean is that you daren't say. Naturally I don't blame you. You've got your job to consider. But you know, my editor would be prepared to pay—"

"Oh, now really, that's *too* much," Corinne interrupted. "I'm not open to bribery."

"Come on now, don't let's use bad words. If you don't want to do it, all right." Isa smiled briefly "I had to try. It's my job to get information."

"And my job is to—"

"To help inflict an unwanted motorway on us?"

"Don't put words in my mouth." Corinne looked round rather wildly for help. Would it be noticeable if she got up and stalked away? Would other people put a wrong construction on it? Would Isa use it against her somehow?

Her eye caught Duncan's. He was listening, chin on fist, to something that was being said by a gaunt lady in a black velvet dress. He frowned, his attention taken by Corinne's distress.

A moment later, after a word of apology, he had left his friends and come to join them.

"Good evening, ladies," he said. "You don't mind if I use you as an excuse to play truant from my protest group?"

68

"Good evening," Corinne said. "Nice to see you."

Surprisingly, this was true. They hadn't exchanged a word since that evening two weeks ago when she accused him of being a trickster.

Their coffee arrived. Corinne invited him to have some with them, which he accepted. Corinne was thankful for his presence as a means of diverting Isa from her attack—although her thankfulness proved short-lived.

"Corinne's just been telling me that the outlook isn't too bright for the anglers," Isa said.

"Isa! I said no such thing."

"You said you didn't blame them for objecting."

"But that's a very different thing from—"

"You mustn't take Isa so seriously," Duncan broke in. "Don't forget she comes from a long line of Border Raiders. It's second nature to her to harry the opposition."

"But I'm not the opposition," Corinne protested. "I'm more or less an innocent bystander!"

"Oh, innocent bystanders were rather badly treated by Border raiders too. In fact," Duncan added, raising an ironic eyebrow at Isa, "even their friends couldn't be sure of coming off unharmed."

"Meaning I've 'harried' you?" Isa said.

"Haven't you? You're absolutely dying to hear I've agreed to be chairman of a protest organization—"

"I can't understand why you won't, Duncan. You know that—"

"I don't *know* anything yet. I haven't many facts, and the few I have are thanks to Corinne." He gave a little bow of acknowledgement to her. "All I can state with certainty is that the Ministry of Highways and the County Council are proposing a motorway. Where it's to run, and whether it's a good thing or a bad thing for the community, I don't yet know."

"Do you have to be so dispassionate?" Isa groaned. "There are no headlines to be got out of logical pros and cons."

"Too bad." There was no sympathy in his voice. "I know it's your ambition to start a big newspaper campaign and be nominated Journalist of the Year, Isa, but don't use other people's anxieties as the framework. Look at poor Corinne—I could see you were nagging at her for something."

"I was not nagging! What an expression!" Isa pouted. "I was inviting her to share my flat with me, that's all. She's coming to look at it the day after tomorrow."

Duncan couldn't conceal his surprise. "You're moving out of the Burney House?"

Corinne admitted she was. "Mr. Eldin feels it's a bit expensive, and of course it is, as a permanent address. It's no part of my conditions of employment that the firm pays for a hotel room. I was looking for a small flat, but to tell the truth there aren't any—most of them are jolly big. People in these parts built such *big* rooms!"

"Yes, the town houses are generally a bit lofty. I quite see that you'd feel lost and overwhelmed all by yourself in a place meant for a family of six."

"She'll like my place," Isa interposed. "You know how nice it is, Duncan."

"It's certainly very trendy inside."

"I'm sure it's very nice," Corinne murmured, wondering if she sounded as unenthusiastic as she felt.

Duncan's friends from across the room drifted over, and a general conversation ensued. By and by Corinne was able to slip away, thus avoiding any further cross-examination by Isa. In her room she watched television for a while, did her nails, and went to bed reflecting that life in Burney was divided between periods of tranquillity such as this and incidents of alarm such as the encounter with Isa or the accident at Catherine's Tower. There seemed to be no halfway measures!

She was just finishing the day's letters next afternoon when her phone rang.

"May I speak to Miss Lenwood?" said a quiet, thin voice.

"Miss Lenwood speaking."

"I thought it was. This is Mrs. Moffat—do you remember me?"

Corinne was astonished to hear her, but very pleased. "Of *course* I do, Mrs. Moffat! How are you?"

"Ach, old—and getting older. My dear, I hear you're looking for a place to live?"

"Good heavens, how did you hear that?"

"Hereabouts, Miss Lenwood, we all tell each other the news. It's true, is it no?"

"That I'm looking for digs? Yes."

"Well now, child, it so happens I've a wee cottage that might please you."

"A cottage!"

"Now, now, don't be expecting great things. It's a shepherd's cottage, nothing but two rooms, but I've modernized it for letting to fishermen, ye see, and it might be a nest that you'd settle into. Would you care to come and see it?"

"But that's so kind of you, Mrs. Moffat! I never expected—"

"Child, don't get hopes too high. You might not take

to it. But I thought I'd just put it in your mind as an idea."

"How do I get there, Mrs. Moffat?"

"Ah, there's the problem. Ye have no car of your own?"

"Not at the moment."

"How would it be if I came and collected you from your office this evening and drove you here? Then afterwards maybe you'd have your evening meal with me. Would that suit you?"

Corinne was delighted with the whole plan. It occupied her thoughts to such an extent that when she took Trav's letters in for his signature she couldn't help saying, "I've been offered a cottage, Trav."

"A cottage? In Hawick?"

"No, on a farm in Caithdale. Have you met Mrs. Moffat? She's a bit of a local celebrity."

"Can't say I have. What's she celebrated for?"

"She's a water-diviner. I saw her on the Hamiltons' farm—"

"Oh, really, Corinne, don't talk such nonsense. Water-diviner indeed!"

"But it's true, Trav—I saw her. She found water twelve feet down in a field."

"She probably knew beforehand that it was there to find, from a map or something."

Corinne paused. Was it all just a trick? "All the local people believe in her."

"More fools they. You know there's no scientific basis for all that stuff, Corinne. And when investigations are carried out you always find that fifty per cent of it is jiggery-pokery, and a lot of the rest isn't substantiated."

"Oh." She hardly knew what to say now. On that afternoon two weeks ago, when she had watched the

72

group in the field, there had been a cheerful matter-of-factness about it that guaranteed its reliability. And Isabel Armstrong had accepted it all as reliable. "That girl from the *Messenger*—she said that—"

"She'll go along with anything that makes a good story. But never mind—it doesn't matter if Mrs. Moffat believes in a flat earth or little green men from Mars, so long as she has a decent place to let. What's it like?"

"I haven't seen it yet. I'll tell you tomorrow."

"You're going this evening? I'll come with you, then."

Corinne hesitated. "Mrs. Moffat is coming to fetch me and giving me dinner later. I'm afraid it's not quite convenient—"

"You mean to say you're friends with her?"

"Not exactly, but I like her—"

"Corinne, is that wise? Do you think you should get on terms like that with these locals?"

"I don't exactly see why not."

"Dad did tell you, didn't he, to tread carefully?"

"But that doesn't mean I can't make friends, surely?"

"It means you have to choose carefully—"

"But you and your father have made friends here. You've been invited out—"

"Yes, but by people we need to cultivate, influential people—"

"Mrs. Moffat is influential!"

"In the wrong way, if you ask me. She sounds a bit of a crank."

Corinne was tempted to say, "She was born a Faa, of the gypsy tribe, and she'll put a *spell* on you if you talk about her like that!" But she didn't think Trav was in the mood to find it funny. So she said, "She's a very nice old lady and her offer is providential, because if I don't find anything else I may be trapped into sharing Isabel Armstrong's flat."

"Heaven forbid!" Trav exclaimed. "Marvellous though that girl is in many ways—good-looking and clever—she's a menace. You'd better take Mrs. Moffat's cottage."

"I want to, if I can."

When she saw it in the early evening sunlight Corinne felt drawn to it. It really was a tiny place, nestling on a south-facing slope with a view of a brook. There was no garden, no fence—the moors came right up to the door, which was of stout old oak, unpainted. The outside made no concessions to the picturesque; it was built of grey stone, had a blue slate roof, and very small windows with plain white-painted frames. The only touch of colour was the bright yellow curtains.

Mrs. Moffat led her in. The front door opened straight into the kitchen-living-room, which had white paint over the rough surface of the uneven walls. Modern electric cooking equipment was housed in a corner screened by a room-divider of bleached pine; the rest of the area held two comfortable armchairs covered in brown linen, a convertible settee in yellow tweed, and a dining arrangement of settle table and benches.

"This way." The other room was the bedroom. One wall had been given over to fitted cupboards and dressing-table; a door in the opposite wall gave access to an extension, recently added, which turned out to be a pretty bathroom tiled in rose pink.

"It's just what we call a but-and-ben," Mrs. Moffat said, "that's to say, a kitchen and bedroom. I haven't done more than I had to in altering it because I didn't want to make it an eyesore with glass verandahs and that kind of nonsense. Besides, anglers only want a place to sleep, they're kind o' fanatical about being out on the water all day."

"I think it's lovely," Corinne said in complete sincerity. "But there's one big problem—how would I get back and forward to the office?"

"You'd need a car," the old lady admitted. "There is a bus hard by, but it's only an hourly service and if ever you missed it, it's a long wait to the next one." She paused. "You can drive?"

"Yes, but in London it was so difficult about parking and so forth that I didn't bother to have a car."

Nothing more was said for the moment. Corinne wandered about, looking in cupboards and trying the switches. The more she saw, the more she felt drawn to the place. That in itself was inexplicable, because she had never imagined herself living so far off the beaten track, yet the cottage seemed home to her the moment she set foot in it.

"It's 'meant'," Mrs. Moffat said as they got back into her aged Wolseley. "The place is right for you."

"But travelling is still a problem."

"You'll find that will solve itself," Mrs. Moffat returned in a tone of absolute conviction.

They had a pleasant meal in her farmhouse, which proved to be a smaller place than the Hamiltons'. She explained that she farmed only sheep and that her husband—"Dead and gone these thirty years, and I miss him still, my dear"—had never needed a big farmhouse to house or feed farm staff. "Shepherds work out in the hills, you understand. My sons lived here, of course, until they married and set up their own homes. One is in New South Wales and another in British Columbia. I have grandchildren scattered all round the world!"

"Don't you get lonely?"

"Never. I've so many friends, including those that work for me. John Staffie, my head shepherd—there's a fine man. And Rona McFee, who comes in to do the house for me, since now I canna scrub floors the way I used to. And mony another, that drops in to have a chat, such as John Staffie's wife. And Duncan, too. He never passes without coming in."

"Duncan Donaldson?" Somehow it didn't surprise her that he should be a friend of the old lady's. There would be an affinity between them, she felt.

She caught the shadow of a smile as Mrs. Moffat said, "You've met him, have you not?"

"Yes, the very first day I arrived." She described how they had almost collided in the mist on Burneybank.

"I'm very fond of Duncan. I knew his father too—a headstrong, lovable man with no head for money. And his mother—she never settled here, alack. It was the town life she loved. When she was widowed Himself made great sacrifices so that she could have all she wanted. And there were the father's debts too . . . Ah well, I mustn't gossip about what's no concern of ours."

Corinne had to accept this, although she would dearly have loved to hear more. When Mrs. Moffat drove her back to the hotel she had arranged to rent the cottage as from the following Saturday at a very reasonable price.

"It will be gorgeous now that summer's coming," she said, "although I don't know if I'd care for it in winter."

"Och, come winter you won't be there," Mrs. Moffat answered.

"Shan't I? But a couple of weeks ago you were predicting it would be many a long day before I went away."

"And that's still true. You'll see, my dear—I'll be proved right on both counts."

Shaking her head, Corinne said goodnight and went indoors. First chance she got tomorrow, she must look for a cheap second-hand car.

She was coming out next morning to wait for Travers and his father to take her into town when Duncan came round the corner from his showroom.

"Good morning, Corinne. Meg Moffat tells me you're on the look-out for a car."

Corinne laughed. "News travels in this neighbourhood with the speed of light!"

"Well, we see no point in not passing it on, particularly if we can be of help to one another. It so happens I have a car for sale that might suit you. Have you time to take a look?"

"I didn't know you sold cars," she said as she fell into step beside him.

"I don't. But this belonged to a friend of mine who's gone abroad. I said I'd try to sell it for her."

Corinne had often strolled past the big open-fronted building where Duncan's agricultural vehicles were on show, but she had never gone in. He led her past two brilliantly coloured tractors and a dump truck, to the area at the back. Here, in a corner, stood a strange little orange-painted car that reminded Corinne of a grasshopper. It was a Mini-moke, rather worn but sturdy.

The first point that occurred to her was that the friend for whom he was selling it must be very young: few elderly ladies drive a Mini-moke.

"The engine's good," Duncan said, "and it's foolproof

where maintenance is concerned. Very manoeuvrable on rough surfaces. What d'you think?"

"I don't know. It's not what I had in mind..."

"It's going cheap. Ever driven one?"

"No."

"Hop in, I'll take you for a spin."

"No, Duncan, Mr. Eldin and Travers will be—"

"Come on—two minutes!" He bundled her in and before she could utter another word they were whizzing out of the yard and out on to the road. Here he slowed to let the morning horse-riders go by.

A girl turned in her saddle as they passed. "So that's why you weren't out this morning!"

He raised a hand in salute but made no reply. Off they went again, at a neat turn of speed—round the back of the hotel, down a track leading to the village, through the main street, and back to the front lawn of the Burney House.

Corinne enjoyed it enormously. It was exhilarating to bounce over the ruts in the road without slackening speed, to feel the wind pulling her long hair back behind her shoulders. But her enjoyment was damped when she saw that Trav's Citroën was at the entrance, with Trav waiting beside it and his father already seated in the back.

"Next circuit, you take the controls," Duncan suggested, making as if to go round again.

"No! No, no, Duncan, they're waiting for me—"

"Good heavens, another three minutes—"

"No, I daren't! Please take me up to the door."

"What d'you mean, daren't? You're not afraid of them?"

"Duncan, be reasonable! Mr. Eldin pays my salary."

"Ah yes," he sighed, turning in between the stone

pillars, "it always comes back to finance in the end, doesn't it, Corinne? I know how you feel . . ."

He took the drive at a sedate pace, out of respect for the Pattersons' gravel, but all the same the contrast between the two cars was extreme, the one so smooth and comfortably cushioned, the other scarcely more than a box on wheels.

She got down in haste as Travers moved impatiently. "I'll let you know this evening," she promised.

"Very well." He nodded in greeting to Travers and drove away again.

"Come along, Corinne, this is no time to go joy-riding," Norman Eldin said.

"I wasn't exactly joy-riding," she protested as she obeyed. "I'm looking for a car to buy."

"Indeed?"

"I've taken a cottage about a mile along this road but off a track among the moors. Public transport isn't—"

"That sounds a bit remote, my dear. A cottage, you say?"

"It is a little isolated. That's why I felt I must have wheels."

"But not *that* contraption, I hope?"

"Y . . . yes, I was rather thinking—"

"No, no, Corinne, a most unsuitable form of transport. Very undignified."

"But do you think that matters—?"

"I shouldn't like to think of a member of my firm gadding about in a thing like that—should you, Travers?"

"If you needed a car why didn't you come to me for advice?" Travers said over his shoulder. "I don't see the necessity of going to Donaldson, of all people!"

"I didn't exactly go to him. He heard I was on the look-out for something not too expensive and this morning he—"

"Not really appropriate, I feel," Mr. Eldin said. "I would much rather you had something with more dignity. Besides, in bad weather you'd find it very cold."

"I believe there's a top that goes over—"

"A small saloon car would be much more suitable. I think we might even make one available to you at the firm's expense, my dear. I think that would be quite in order, don't you, Travers?"

"We're already running this car and the Land-Rovers for the survey team, Dad."

"So we are. However, I expect the accountants can sort it out if we advance Corinne the money to buy a little car—a Viva or a Minx, what?"

Corinne had mixed feelings. She couldn't exactly disagree that the Mini-moke was impractical, but she had an idea that the price would be very reasonable indeed. That appealed to her more than going into debt over a car that would please Mr. Eldin.

"Might I think it over?"

Travers said in a displeased tone, "I'm amazed that you hesitate, Corinne. I quite see that you want to take the cottage if it's comfortable and cheap, but that's enough spur-of-the-moment action for the present. It would be idiotic to saddle yourself with that buggy, when my father's making you this rather generous offer."

It dawned on her that it could create an awkwardness if she refused. Travers would have to bear the brunt of his father's displeasure. She gave in at once and Mr. Eldin, who was not an ungenerous man, arranged to go with her at lunchtime to pick up something " 'rich, not gaudy', as it says in Hamlet."

So that evening she found herself driving back in a little pale blue Renault, a very ladylike little car chosen by her employer. When she drew up neatly in the drive she was proud of it yet rather uncertain : the debt would have to be paid off over a long time and though the car was not new it was certainly a lot more expensive than that useful little vehicle that Duncan had offered.

She had to go and see him. She went round to the showroom, which was now closed; she rang the bell for the upstairs apartment. She heard the clatter of his shoes on the wooden staircase. A moment later the door opened to reveal Duncan with a sheaf of papers in his hand.

"Ah, I was expecting you! Come up and have some sherry—"

"No, Duncan. I only came to—"

"Come along, that wind will carry away my account slips." He took it for granted that she would follow as he led the way upstairs.

His home was in many ways an expression of the man—the long loft had been divided up into rooms floored with polished teak on which rough Scandinavian rugs were scattered. Cabinets with papers and books lined the room into which he showed her. There was a desk, and a long bench with a microscope and a plant-press, and a group of comfortable chairs.

"Sit down?" he invited.

"No, thank you. Duncan, I've really only come to say that I've decided against the Mini-moke."

"Oh. I thought you were rather taken with it?"

"I was, but it really isn't suitable. Mr. Eldin felt quite strongly that it would be a bad choice."

"And his opinion matters so much?"

"Well . . ." She hesitated, wishing she could explain the situation in few words. "He made me a very generous offer to help me get a car, and he's the kind of person who doesn't like to take no for an answer."

"Are you telling me you've got to do what Mr. Eldin says because otherwise he gets annoyed?" he said in a tone of cold surprise.

"More or less . . . yes." She added after half a second's pause, "I don't mind so much for myself, but Travers has to bear the brunt of it."

She was looking down at the mellow brown of the wooden floor, but she could feel his gaze upon her. When he said nothing, she looked up. She felt sure that what she saw on his face was scorn mixed with pity.

"I quite understand," he said formally. "Thank you for letting me know you're not interested in the Moke."

There was no more to be said. She was about to go when, urged by a desire to get back on a better footing with him, she plunged into speech again, using the first thought that came into her head.

"What's the microscope for?"

"I beg your pardon?" He was taken aback.

"The microscope on the bench . . ." She moved towards that instead of towards the door. He was too well-mannered to show any impatience. She went on: "Do you look at flowers through a microscope?"

"Hardly." She could hear amusement in the word and wondered if, should she look round with a smile, he would smile back. Better not to risk it . . . She put out a hand, and he said hastily, "Please don't touch! I've got a root-system section in the holder—"

"A root-system . . ."

"No, no, only a tiny piece—" He broke off. "Are you really interested or only making conversation?"

Corinne knew she was blushing. "I suppose . . . only making conversation. But I didn't realize you used a microscope. It's sort of impressive!"

"How absurd," he replied, breaking into a smile. "A microscope is no more impressive than a pair of binoculars."

"But it means you're very immersed in the subject. After all, that—" she nodded at the instrument—"must be quite an expensive thing."

"That's true. But so is hi-fi equipment, or a sailing dinghy—it's just a question of where one's interest lies."

"And you're interested in plants."

"Always have been. I used to keep leaves between the pages of my school books."

"So did I, I believe," she said, her face lighting up. "Autumn leaves, all gorgeous colours . . ."

"What's your hobby, Corinne?" he asked. "What are you interested in?"

She was rather ashamed at the list she brought out. "We—ell . . . the theatre, and films, and . . . and clothes . . ."

He laughed. "What are you going to find to do with your spare time hereabouts?"

"Now I've got my own transport I'll be able to go into Edinburgh—"

"Oh yes, the car. You've already got it?"

"Yes, a little Renault. Mr. Eldin chose it at lunch-time."

"For the love of Pete, Corinne, haven't you any will of your own?" he demanded, suddenly taking her by the shoulders. "You *came* here because the firm sent you, you *do* as the firm tells you—do you do anything out of your own free will?"

She could see the impatience in his expression, feel it in the grip of his fingers through her silk dress. *Was* she too docile? She looked up at him, unwittingly appealing for his tolerance.

The irritation died out of his eyes, to be replaced by something she couldn't identify. "You really are the most extraordinarily pretty girl," he murmured.

She knew he was going to kiss her. She knew she should evade it. But it seemed her body was tied down by a thousand silk threads which prevented her from moving, and transmitted a strange shiver of excitement.

His lips touched hers, gently at first. But next moment a fierce current seemed to pass between them, driving them together in an embrace like fire. Everything was consumed in it. She lost awareness of place or time for that everlasting moment. She couldn't have said how long went by before she wrenched herself away.

"How dare you!" she gasped, breathless and indignant.

He looked down at her, a strange glint in the slate-blue eyes. "What's the matter?" he enquired. "Are you afraid Mr. Eldin or his son would disapprove?"

"That's not the point! I—" But she didn't quite know what it was she wanted to say; her senses were in confusion.

Bereft of words, she turned and hurried out, almost stumbling down the steep staircase in her anxiety to get away.

CHAPTER FIVE

AS if he sensed that Corinne needed his help and support, Travers began to spend more time with her. He helped her move into the cottage and took her to Edinburgh to buy a few additional items—cushions and lampshades and flower-vases. He was very worried for fear she would be lonely in her new home; he took her for picnics and to visit gourmet restaurants in the evenings. They went sightseeing at weekends : Corinne began to think there were more ruined abbeys, castles and battlefields round Burney than anywhere else in the world—but she enjoyed it, for in fine weather this was a beautiful landscape, green and smiling, with the dancing waters of a trout stream round almost every curve of the hills.

Driven on, perhaps, by her feeling of inadequacy when Duncan had asked her what she was interested in, Corinne took up riding. She had had one or two lessons in London, jogging round a common in company with a flatmate who was keen. But now she applied herself seriously under old Mrs. Moffat's approving eye. The riding school was run by an elderly man, David Inglis, who seemed possessed of inexhaustible patience and a conviction, for which at first Corinne could see no justification, that she was a natural horsewoman.

But as May passed into June and June into July she began to gain confidence in her own ability. The little Border ponies used for hill-trekking were so surefooted, so reliable, that really all you needed to do was sit in the saddle—the pony did the rest. She grew fond of her mount, a little chestnut mare called Minty.

The various common-ridings began to take place; she

and Travers drove to watch the Hawick Riding, the Peebles Beltane Fair, the Melrose Festival, the Galashiels Braw Lads, the Jedburgh Callants. In mid-July came the Burney Ride-out.

Made ambitious by her progress as a horsewoman, Corinne said to her riding instructor: "Could I follow the Ride-out on horseback?"

David Inglis shook his head. "No, no, dear lady. The Burney event turns into a bit of a steeplechase on the way back. I'd advise you to stay in the village and watch them come home with the banners flying."

"But that seems so tame, Mr. Inglis! Travers and I have been to watch at several and everybody's having such fun. Now that it's going to be Burney's turn, I feel I've got a right to take part."

"Miss Lenwood, you really must not. It's all right for people brought up in these hills to tear down a slope like an express train, but if you tried it you'd be unseated." Hearing her sigh, he relented a little. "I'll tell you what. On the day of the Ride-out you can come out with me. I'm taking part, but perhaps I'm getting too old to keep up with the Standard-bearer."

"Do you mean it?" Corinne cried. "That would be marvellous!"

Corinne had seen enough of the various ceremonies to have picked up some general knowledge about them. In essence they were a mixture of pageantry and physical prowess. Each town had a slightly different version, but usually things began with beating the bounds of the parish, in ceremonial dress and with a mounted band in attendance. Then there would be some historical event to commemorate—the protecting of the town against attack, or a foray against some old enemy which had resulted in heroic deeds.

The Burney tradition centred round the Standard-bearer. In the days before Mary Stuart a company of men had gone out to join their king in battle. All had been slain, but one by one they had handed on their flag to a survivor until, at last, the only remaining soldier had ridden home to place it on the steps of the village market cross with his dying breath. Tradition had it that he had been pursued closely, so the Burney Ride-out ended with a furious gallop back from the hills to the centre of the village.

The Standard-bearer for this year was a boy from a farm beyond the Caith Water, already well-known for his success at gymkhanas and horse shows. When Corinne trotted up on Minty, he was already at the market cross, looking quite different from the tumbled-haired lad she had seen so many times. He was wearing a dark green loden jacket with a matching cap rather like a tam-o'-shanter, but with a long pheasant's feather trailing from it. Behind him was a line of mounted men, many of them in jackets of the same cloth, though not the cap.

"Do they buy them specially?" Corinne whispered to Mr. Inglis.

"Buy them? My word, no—they're given to them by the village of Burney. Each one has been a Standard-bearer in his time, ye see."

"But suppose they out-grow them?" she teased.

"Then they have the seams let out till they fall to pieces!" He went on to mention one or two of his friends who owned Burney jackets, but Corinne was no longer listening.

Among the mounted entourage she had glimpsed a familiar figure. "Isn't that Duncan Donaldson?"

"Aye, he never misses. He was Standard-bearer in . . . now let me see . . . it was the year before his father passed on." Mr. Inglis grinned, rubbing his weathered cheek with his forefinger. "*He* led us a ride, I can tell you! He was a furlong ahead of the rest of us when we came back, going like the wind. I mind I got a whack on the cheek from a birch tree, trying to keep up with him through the wood. Aye, aye," sighed the riding-master, "that was before he had to tackle all the debts and the problems . . ."

The minister handed the standard up to the Standard-bearer, who accepted it with solemnity. Then the whole concourse clattered off to pace out the parish boundaries. At the front went the Standard-bearer and the men; women riders were expected to keep well back, for this was a commemoration of an exclusively male episode. Behind the horses came a few followers in cars or on foot. Travers was there in the Citroën, interested to watch Corinne take part in this ceremony.

Sedately the procession wound its way along the quiet roads, the flag glinting at the front—a five-petalled rose in white on a field of azure, bordered in gold. At the milestones there would be a pause and a flourish of trumpets. Finally the Standard-bearer headed up a stony track, leaving the cars on the road along with most of the pedestrians. The path led up to the crest of the hills, beyond Burneybank to the far side of the Caith river. It was from here that the race began, but it was a race with no set race-track, for in memory of the heroic survivor hunted by his pursuers the Standard-bearer would choose the most difficult route he could.

The silver trumpets sounded. The Standard-bearer

raised his flag and then, like an arrow from a bow, launched himself and his horse into a headlong gallop along the hillside. His "pursuers" had to wait for the signal to follow, which came three minutes later. With a wild yell almost a hundred and fifty people went careering in his tracks.

David Inglis had no intention of joining in when first he set out with Corinne. But the temptation was too much for him. With a glance of agonized apology at Corinne, he took off after the rest of the field.

Corinne's mount took it for granted that she belonged with the rest. She went thudding off after them. Corinne, taken by surprise, was jolted about for the first few yards. But she regained control without too much trouble and after the first few excited minutes the little mare began to slack off : she was no match for the big chestnut up at the front, nor was she being urged on by her rider. She fell back. By and by the rest of the field had streamed away out of sight into the next glen.

Corinne cantered after them, just in time to see them splashing through a ford about half a mile to the east below her. She followed on and took the ford. The tracks went in a broad swathe over the wet ground, showing the direction to take. She let the mare pick her way over the slippery surface without haste, reflecting as she did so that in the first place it was rather foolish to follow on because from now on she would be riding all by herself, and in the second place she wasn't sure if she could face the various hazards that the Standard-bearer had in mind.

She drew rein at the top of the next slope, debating whether to turn back. Then she saw a horseman further along the ridge, silhouetted like an Indian in a Western. As she studied him, he flagged with his arm and turned his horse towards her. She saw, as he came nearer, that it was Duncan.

"Hello there. I guessed you were on your own when I saw David streaming up to the front of the pursuit."

"Hello," she replied, slightly perplexed. "Why aren't you alongside David?"

He shrugged. "It's good fun, but it's not the most important thing in the world. Besides—" and he laughed—"that young devil is going to make them cross the Caith Water under the waterfall, and they'll all get soaked."

"I don't think I'd like that," she admitted.

"What are you going to do?"

"I don't know. Make my way back, I suppose."

"Mind if I join you?"

Since the episode of the kiss, she had been avoiding him. Whether it was because she was angry or embarrassed, she could not decide. She had seen him at the Burney House Hotel once or twice when she dined there with Travers, and more than once he had driven past her cottage, on his way to see Mrs. Moffat. But on the whole they had not seen each other.

Now, however, she experienced a great sense of pleasure at his presence. She told herself that it was because riding all alone wasn't much fun.

He fell in beside her. Under his guidance they set off down the slope into the next valley and from there by a gentle, ambling track back to the Burneybank.

"That's where we first came upon each other," he said, pointing up the hillside.

"I remember. What a fright you gave me!" She

smiled in recollection and then added, "What were you doing that day? Were you collecting something special?"

"Something special, yes. But I wasn't collecting. It's too precious to be picked."

"Really?" she cried, immediately intrigued. "What was it? A flower, or a grass, or what?"

"A flower. Very rare. It only grows in about three places in the British Isles, and until I reported its presence here in April, it had never been known in the Borders."

"But, Duncan, that's absolutely wonderful!" She was thrilled at the idea. "What flower is it? Can you tell me?"

"Well . . . it's an orchid."

"An *orchid*? In Scotland? But I thought they were tropical plants!"

They had stopped now so as to talk. He said, "You're picturing a huge lilac-coloured blossom like those you see in a florist's window. Wild orchids are quite different, at least in this country. They're smaller and less showy."

"I can't believe it. Orchids? Here?" She swept her hand out in a gesture that took in the cool green of the valley.

"Quite a few grow here. The purple orchid, the spotted orchid, the bird's-nest, and one with the odd name of twayblade."

"And which is it that you've found?"

"None of those. I told you, it's very rare. It's a pretty little thing, creamy white, with a lovely scent—particularly at night."

"Oh, I remember! That night you rescued me at

Catherine's Tower—you said you were going to look at a night-scented flower."

"Yes, but not this one. This blooms in August—and it takes years to settle down in a new place and come into flower."

"And is that what's happened? It's come into flower?"

He looked as if he rather regretted having told her about it.

"May I see it?" she begged. "Please—I'd love to."

Duncan hesitated. "It's rather special," he said. "I haven't told anyone about it except the Botanical Society." Then, seeing her disappointment: "All right, we'll go. But we'll have to lead the horses."

They dismounted and, with the reins over their arms, went on foot along the valley, then up the hill to a point very near the long thicket of burnet roses. These had nearly ended their blooming: only a few pale flowers reflected back the sunshine.

" 'Tis the last rose of summer,

Left blooming alone . . .' " Corinne murmured as they paused to look.

"Yes, but at least you can be certain the burnet rose will be back next year. Now with the orchid . . ." He shook his head. "It may take ten or fifteen years to get established and to produce a blossom. Then next year when you come back—not a flower in sight. Leaves and roots, but no blossoms."

"But why not?"

"Oh, they're easily upset. A slight change in the environment. There was a colony of marsh helleborine doing quite well a few miles from the village, but it disappeared when the owner of the land put in drainage ditches, and that was quite some distance away."

"They sound temperamental," she said, smiling.

"Fastidious is the word. And a bit mysterious."

"I can hardly wait to see this one."

"You mustn't expect anything tremendous to look at," he said, rather anxiously. "Let's tether the horses here. It's only a few yards now."

It was, in fact, the marsh where Corinne had left a shoe. But today she was sensibly shod in riding-boots so that she was able to follow without demur as he led the way.

"Here it is," he said, bending to separate the sedge grass.

She saw a spike of flowers standing up among the grasses. They were closely placed about the stem, the petals a rich creamy white and like narrow bells. As she stooped to look at it, a wave of perfume came up to meet her, a scent of depth and smoothness that reminded her of vanilla yet was subtly different.

"What is it called?" she asked in a hushed voice.

"Ladies' tresses."

"Oh, how lovely! What a *beautiful* name!"

He wrinkled his nose in amusement. "The Latin name is Spiranthes romanzoffiana!"

"Why, I think that's almost as good. Romanzoffiana! It sounds like a Russian ballerina. But I like ladies' tresses better."

"So do I. I always prefer the common name for a plant."

"But how can this have a 'common' name if it's so rare?"

"Rare in this country. It's found quite often in America."

"So how did it get here?"

"Who knows?" he said, letting the curtain of grass

93

come together around it. "I told you—orchids are mysterious!"

They went down the hill again, and on towards the village without remounting. Their conversation interested Corinne so much that she wanted it to continue; she encouraged him to talk about his hobby and through that, about his life.

She learned that he had always been interested in plants, but the interest had been reinforced by a wish to understand and help the countryside in which he lived. The crops that the farms produced, the vegetation that nourished the flocks—these had been subjects for study. She had a feeling that his family had owned land: she remembered that one or two people had spoken of his father's death as if it had brought great changes. But he didn't mention this. Instead he described how the parts of his life fitted together—the business side of supplying agricultural transport, the hobby of observing and protecting the land, and ancillary activities on committees of various kinds.

She realized that, though she had always imagined living in the country to be quiet and secluded, almost the opposite was true—here people were more closely knit, more closely involved. Duncan's life was just as full and busy as Mr. Eldin's; the difference was that for him money was not the motivating force, nor was the pursuit of power.

They came strolling into the village in mid-afternoon, when all the Standard-bearer's party had been back for over an hour and the whole population had sat down to the open-air meal that was the momentary break in today's celebrations. Space was made for them at one of the long tables. Without further thought Corinne was about to sit down, when an angry voice broke in.

"So there you are! Do you realize I've been worried sick about you?"

It was Travers, looking dark with anger. Corinne was too astonished to make any reply.

"You've been missing for *hours*!" he accused, looking from her to Duncan and back again. "I hadn't a clue where you were!"

"Didn't Mr. Inglis tell you what happened?"

"He told me he left you up on the ridge by the Caith Water, but that meant you'd have been back at three if you'd ridden directly home."

"Well . . . I didn't. I . . . went to . . ." She caught Duncan's eye and broke off just as she was about to say she'd been to look at an orchid.

"It's my fault, I'm afraid," Duncan said. "I delayed Corinne—"

"What I don't understand is how you came to be with her in the first place. Everyone expected you to come in on the heels of the Standard-bearer." Travers was too angry to stop himself; if he could have heard himself he would have realized he was handling the situation badly, but his anger deafened his ears to his own tone.

Heads were turning. Some faces showed amusement, some embarrassment. There were one or two murmurs of "Sit down, man!"

Corinne said, "Trav, I'm sorry if you were worried. It didn't occur to me that—"

"That's what I'm complaining about," he broke in.

The villagers sitting at the table raised their voices in protest. Corinne's main wish was to end the scene before it became even more embarrassing. Instead of sitting down at the space on the bench which had been

95

made for her and Duncan, she took Travers by the arm and drew him away.

"Come and talk to me," she murmured.

"Och, sit ye down, lassie!" exclaimed Mrs. Hamilton from her place at the table. "You'll miss the fun!"

Corinne hesitated. Her eye caught Duncan's. He made a little gesture of invitation towards the seat that was awaiting her beside him. She had a sense that it was something of an honour—there was a look of expectancy on the faces of the others which seemed to imply 'She *can't* refuse'.

But Travers had taken her wrist in a grip of steel. "You said we were going for a walk!" he said.

"Yes, I'm coming." Though she said it to Travers, her gaze was on Duncan.

She saw the disdain come into his eyes. Colouring painfully, she went with Travers away from the merriment in the Market Square, along the deserted village street.

Scarcely had they moved out of sight of the others when she found herself swept into his arms, and felt his kisses on her cheeks and her eyelids and, finally, her mouth.

"Corinne!" he muttered. "Never do a thing like that to me again!"

"But, Trav—"

"I was so humiliated! Kicking my heels there by the Market Cross, wondering where the dickens you were! Have you any idea of the kind of thing that was being said by the village gossip?"

"What kind of thing? I don't understand, Trav—"

"Oh, don't be so naïve! They thought you were off in some cosy nook with Duncan."

"With Duncan?" She gasped. "But that's nonsense!"

"You *were* with him."

"Well, yes. No one denies that. But it was just that he rather kindly turned back when all the others streamed off after the Standard-bearer."

"That's the whole point! They were saying it was very odd that he hadn't arrived, and someone reported he'd turned back for you, and they all laughed and looked knowing."

"Trav! They didn't!"

"They certainly did. And said he wasn't the sort to waste his time."

"Oh no! No, you must have got it wrong!" She was so distressed that her eyes filled with tears, ready to spill over. "No, Trav, you've made a mistake. After all, they'd be speaking Lallands and you know you don't understand—"

"I understood the way they chuckled when your name was mentioned. That was easy to understand in *any* language."

She blinked hard to get rid of the tears. "How dare they!"

"Oh, in a little place like this, what else do you expect? You know we've already had a taste of the way news or rumour flies around."

"But they've no right—"

He shook his head at her, rather reproachfully. "Come now, darling, you did rather ask for it. After all, this isn't the first time you've been linked with that fellow—"

"I don't know what you mean, 'linked'—"

"You haven't forgotten you nearly let him talk you into buying that absurd beach-buggy contraption? There you were, whizzing round the village in it. And

97

then everybody knows that it's thanks to you he got the information about the motorway—"

"But that was my very first day here. They couldn't imagine there was anything between us in that short time."

"Why not? How long does it take for a man and a woman to feel attracted to each other? Besides, ever since then you've been living in that creepy little cottage at the back of beyond, and everybody knows he drives out in that direction quite often."

"Travers!" Corinne was too shocked to say anything more.

He sounded uncomfortable as he went on. "I'm not saying there's anything in it . . ."

"It's being said by the people of the village?"

"No—o . . . Nothing's being *said* . . ."

Her mind began to function again. "Good gracious, Trav, they must all know perfectly well that he goes straight past my cottage. He's visiting Mrs. Moffat at her farm."

"I suppose they—"

"Look here," she interrupted, her dismay beginning to diminish as she thought about it, "is the real truth that *you* have been thinking these things?" She stared up at him. "Are you putting words into other people's mouths?"

"Corinne . . ."

"Please be honest with me, Trav. Have you been imagining some sort of relationship between Duncan and me?"

Flushing with annoyance, he replied: "Are you saying there's nothing between you?"

It was only a momentary hesitation before she spoke.

She had to banish the memory of that one kiss. "Nothing," she said.

"On *your* side," he insisted. "But what about him?"

"Honestly, Trav, I think he . . . rather despises me!" She couldn't have explained why it hurt so much to say that.

"Oh yes, of course!" Travers said in utter disbelief. "That's why he turned back today when you were left on your own."

"In a way . . . yes, that's why. He felt a bit responsible for me because he regards me as not very suited to the life at Burney. I suppose he felt I might get lost up there in the hills."

Travers looked unconvinced, but said. "At least as far as you're concerned, you don't feel any special interest in him?"

"Oh, I don't know if I can say that, Trav. He is a very interesting man. He was telling me about the plants on the hillside—"

"Plants?" Travers exclaimed, on a burst of amusement. "*That's* what you were talking about?"

"Yes, that's his special hobby—" She broke off, having been on the verge of mentioning the bench microscope she had seen in Duncan's room. That was best forgotten, together with the rest of that episode.

Travers didn't notice her abrupt stop. His good humour completely restored, he gave her a little kiss on the tip of the nose. "Darling, I'm sorry I got so worked up. You do realize, don't you, that it was because I was worried in case something had happened to you?"

"I understand."

"What I wish," he went on, leading her with his arm around her towards his car, "is that you and I could get engaged. Then Donaldson would understand there's a 'No Trespassing' sign on you."

"Oh, darling, that's not very agreeable," she said, divided between a feeling of hurt and amusement. "I'm not a piece of property."

"Yes, you are—you're my property!" He gave her a little hug. "You are, aren't you?"

"Am I?" she countered.

"Don't you feel that? That you belong to me, just as I belong to you?"

They had reached his Citroën. She paused at its side. She was perplexed at being unable to answer an immediate yes to his question. "Travers," she said slowly, "is anything ever going to come of it?"

She felt him stiffen. He took his arm away. After a moment he said, "You think I'm a coward, don't you? Because I won't face up to my father about you."

"I didn't say that."

"But it's what you mean. I suppose, like every other girl, you want to have a ring to show off and—"

"Trav!" she interrupted. "When have I ever mentioned any such thing?"

"Well, you haven't actually said it, but it's only natural you should be thinking it.

She said with some coldness : "You're putting words into other people's mouths again. But since you yourself have raised the issue, let's talk about it. You say you feel I belong to you just as you belong to me. You want to have rights over choosing my friends. Oh—" she held up a hand as he was about to intervene—"I'm not concerned over being friends or not with Duncan. That's not what I'm talking about. All I want to know is, if I give you those rights—if I let you monopolize me, Trav—what do I get in exchange?"

When she heard herself say the words she was astounded. Was this Corinne Lenwood? Daring to make an issue of Trav's taking her for granted? In the months since she first met him she had always accepted whatever he said and did as the level at which their relationship was to continue, yet now—all in a moment, it seemed—she was challenging him.

He had turned away as she was speaking, to stare moodily at the whitewashed cottage opposite. There was a lark singing over the pasture behind the village.

At last he said, "What do you expect me to say? You know we can't get married."

"Can't we?" She didn't point out that there was nothing to stop them. They were over eighteen and in full possession of all their faculties.

"You know what I mean. Dad would raise the roof."

"Then what are our prospects?" Once again she was surprised. The words were so clipped and cool. What had given her the courage to bring the issue out into the open like this?

"Well . . . we'll have to wait a bit."

"Until when, Trav?"

"Until a good opportunity arises." He turned back towards her, seized both her hands. "You do see, darling, don't you, that it would hardly be fair to have a big family row just at the moment when he's in the middle of problems here about the by-pass route? It's tricky. He's got to be careful not to put a foot wrong. I couldn't suddenly confront him with the idea of marrying someone he wouldn't approve of."

"But he likes me, darling," she said eagerly. "Look how generous he was about my car."

"Of course he likes you! Who wouldn't?" He gave her a little hug. "But I don't have to spell it out for you. Dad's always envisaged me marrying someone who'll do a bit of good either financially or socially."

"And I don't fit that description," she admitted, although without rancour—she could understand Norman Eldin's ambition for his son.

"I know it sounds mercenary, but try not to hold it against him. When the moment comes to tell him about you, I know he'll accept it. But it's got to be the *right* moment. You do see that, Corinne?"

She nodded. "And in the meantime . . . ?"

For a moment he seemed to hesitate; then with the air of a man taking a plunge into cold water, he said: "We could be engaged!"

"Engaged? But you said—"

"We'll go to Edinburgh the first chance we get, and choose a ring! What would you like, sweetheart? A diamond? A sapphire?"

"But, Trav, what would your father say?" she insisted, baffled at the plan.

"Oh, we wouldn't tell him! It would be unofficial. You and I would be the only ones to know."

"But the ring, Trav?"

"You could wear it when just the two of us go out. It would be our secret!"

"I don't know whether that's a good idea—"

"Of course it is! It'll make a world of difference to us to have taken that step. After all, Corinne, a chap doesn't spend a lot of money on a ring unless he intends to carry the thing through!"

She could see the logic in that. What she couldn't quite pin down was a feeling of disinclination for the whole scheme. But Travers drew her close and murmured, "Please, sweetheart—please say yes! If you do, I'll never feel any uneasiness about you again . . ."

So she agreed they would be engaged.

Unofficially, of course. And she wouldn't get to wear her ring. And the main obstacle—Mr. Eldin senior—was still in her path.

But if it made Trav happy, it was worth it.

CHAPTER SIX

THAT evening the Burney Ride-out Ball was held in the Burney House Hotel. In a way Corinne would rather not have gone, but how would her absence be explained to Mr. Eldin? He had agreed to attend; his decision had had the note of "royal assent"—'I shall grace the event with my presence', he implied. He was quite convinced he was the most important personage in Burney, and Corinne supposed it was true. There was the minister of the church, and the headmaster of the school, and the chairman of the local council—and it was probably true to say that none of them was as influential as Norman Eldin.

Since he would be there, it was more or less inevitable that Travers and Corinne should go too. They were, more or less, his entourage.

Corinne had been warned that this was a very formal affair. She had therefore spent a lot of money on a very beautiful dress of leaf green silk, which set off her russet hair to perfection. Normally, before a ball, she would have gone to a hairdresser for a special hair-do, but as she had spent most of the day riding round the countryside there had been no opportunity. She comforted herself with the thought that most of the other women would be in a similar plight as she combed and brushed her wind-tangled mane; when she had at last tied it back in a simple bow of matching green, it looked demure and pretty.

She set off through the sunny August evening in the Renault, happy enough at the prospect of the dance. It was in her nature to be an optimist. No matter how miserable and perplexed she had been a couple of hours ago she began to feel that, after all, it was the village's yearly celebration—it was bound to be fun.

And so it was. The ballroom at the hotel had been decorated with bunting and coats of arms. A band was installed on the dais, consisting of violin, drums, piano and accordion. As had been foretold, the guests were in their finery; the women almost all in long dresses, and even so being rivalled by some of the men who were in traditional costume. Some wore the kilt, with velvet jacket and lace ruffles. Others wore tartan trews and a dark jacket edged with braid; and there were a few in hunting pink.

All in all, a glittering sight. Corinne felt the last of her depression lift from her spirits, especially as the band was already playing one of her favourite tunes as she came in, a waltz from *The Sound of Music.*

Corinne had taken care not to arrive too early. Among her London friends it was considered unsophisticated to turn up at the hour printed on the ticket. Here, she found this was regarded as eccentric.

"Ye're awfu' late!" remarked Mr. Inglis, her riding instructor, as he bustled up to her in the doorway. "We've been pounding the floor for nearly an hour. Come away in ... And may I have the honour?"

He swept her on to the floor. To her surprise he danced well. They circled in perfect harmony until the tune ended, and then there was a roll of drums.

"Take your partners, ladies and gentlemen, for the first eightsome of the evening!"

There was a shout of acclamation. People began to scurry about.

"What's going on?" Corinne asked, mystified.

"It's an eightsome reel. We'd better join one of the sets—"

"But, Mr. Inglis, I can't dance a reel . . ."

He was paying no attention, but tugged her along at his back. They made their way to the end near the dais, where a group was forming up into a square. "Here we are," Mr. Inglis said with satisfaction, unbuttoning his evening jacket in readiness for exertion. "We'll be able to hear the music fine. Farther up the hall it sometimes gets drowned out by all the stamping and hallooing."

"Mr. Inglis! *Mr. Inglis!*" Corinne said imploringly. "I don't know how to dance this thing."

"What?" He looked taken aback. "What's that you say?"

"I've never danced a reel."

"Never danced a reel?" It was quite clear he regarded this as heresy.

"Oh, they're an uneducated lot in the south," said a well-known voice.

And there, standing on the opposite side of the reel, was Duncan.

"I'd better sit this one out," Corinne said, panicky.

"Nonsense!" cried Isa, appearing at Duncan's side. "All you have to do is follow the rest of us. It's simple really."

105

Corinne was still arguing that she couldn't, and try-ing to wrest her hand from David Inglis, when the band struck up a long chord and they were off. Every-body joined hands and went off in a circle. That seemed easy enough, so she did it. Unexpectedly they stopped and danced as partners, opposite each other. Corinne was momentarily at a loss and had just fathomed what to do when when Mr. Inglis seized her round the waist and swung her to the centre. Luckily Isa was immed-iately opposite, took her hand, and she found she was forming a cross.

So it went on, with Corinne picking it up as move-ment succeeded movement. She was glad when a moment came that gave a chance to rest and summon her wits : one of the girls moved into the centre to dance by her-self while the others circled round and then paused while she danced first with her own partner and then the man facing her. Corinne was just telling herself, as the girl returned to her place, that the tune was coming to an end when—presto—the girl opposite Corinne went into the centre to do her solo.

It dawned on Corinne that each girl must do it in turn. At the moment Isa held the floor; next would come the third girl and then it would be Corinne's turn. She would have to pay attention, or she wouldn't know what to do.

It turned out to be simple enough. Each girl danced first with her own partner, then with the man opposite, and then in a reel of three; after a circle movement, the same girl danced with the other two men in the same way. When it came to Corinne's moment she was able to step forward with a fair amount of confidence.

All went well for the first few steps—she faced David Inglis, turned with him, and then moved to face Duncan.

But at that very moment she looked along the room to the door. Travers and Norman Eldin had just come in—and Travers' face was like a thundercloud as Duncan put his arm around her and swung her round.

"Let me go!" she whispered to Duncan.

He paid no attention, relinquishing his hold only at the moment when he and David Inglis had to pass and re-pass across the square with her. "What's the matter?" he murmured as he went by.

There was no chance to reply. In a moment it was time to dance with the other two men of the set, and she dared to look up in search of Travers. He was nowhere to be seen at present, though.

How utterly infuriating that he should happen along just when she appeared to be flinging herself into Duncan's arms! Truth was, that was the style of the eightsome reel; there was no use dancing it as if it were a minuet. It had a gaiety and a sort of wild simplicity that she had just begun to enjoy when Travers appeared on the scene . . .

The whole process of dancers-in-the-centre had to be repeated again with the men as the soloists. Corinne began to think it would never end, and looked round in apprehension when once again she had to dance alone with Duncan. Her eye found Trav; he was standing with his father, in conversation with Colonel Walker. At least, Mr. Eldin was conversing. Travers was grimly watching the dancers.

"It's absurd!" she told herself. "Where's the harm in dancing with other men?"

That didn't prevent her from being profoundly glad when the reel ended and she was able to make her escape. She threaded her way through the applauding dancers to reach the Eldins.

"Mmm . . ." she said, fanning herself with her little evening bag, "that was hot work!"

"I saw you, my dear, thoroughly enjoying yourself," Mr. Eldin said with approval. "It was an eightsome reel, wasn't it? When I was in the Army and used to go to dances at Highland regiments, they usually included at least one. Rather enjoyed them, I must say! If they have another this evening, perhaps you'll do me the honour, eh, Corinne?"

"I'd love that, Mr. Eldin."

"Good, that's a date." He nudged his son. "She's a credit to the firm, isn't she, Travers?"

"Very pretty," Travers said coolly.

Norman Eldin glanced at him. At first there was surprise at his son's tone and then, perhaps, satisfaction. "Everything seems to be going with a swing," he remarked, nodding at the crowded dance floor. "Rather a pity you and I were an hour late, Travers."

"Oh, I don't suppose they missed us."

"No, I suppose not. You were dancing with Donaldson, weren't you, Corinne?"

"No, actually, my partner was David Inglis," she replied, taking care not to let Travers know that she was speaking very clearly so that he would be sure to hear.

"Inglis? Oh yes, the riding school." Mr. Eldin gave a momentary frown. "That's another one," he said to Travers.

"Another what?" Corinne enquired.

"Nothing, nothing. Just a passing thought." He paused a moment, then added, "What sort of man is he? Has he any influential friends?"

"Mr. Inglis? No, I don't imagine so," Corinne replied, puzzled.

"Neither has Walker," Travers said. "There's no need to worry about him either."

"My dear boy, a man who's been a colonel in a crack regiment can never be entirely without influential friends," his father returned. "And you must realize that he's not by any means the only fisherman . . . Still, there are plenty of other trout streams."

Corinne began to understand what they were referring to: it was like tuning in a radio station—the words began to make sense.

"Are you saying that you've made a final recommendation about the route of the by-pass?"

"Ssh!" said Mr. Eldin, glancing about. "Someone might hear."

"It's confidential?"

"Not exactly. But naturally the planners don't want it talked about until they've got all the problems ironed out." Mr. Eldin nodded in satisfaction. "That's why I wasn't at this pageant thing this morning. I've been having an informal lunch with one of the Ministry chaps. He was very pleased, really, very pleased . . . Not many farmers involved . . . That always causes trouble, if you have to buy up good farmland."

"But you said something about the trout stream . . . ?"

"Oh yes, that'll have to be diverted. Might mean a difference to the fishing, I suppose, but it can't be helped. Otherwise it's more or less easy until it gets to the village."

"This village?"

"Round the back here. What a difference it'll make to their trade! At the moment it's a bit like the back of beyond, isn't it?"

"I think they like it that way," Corinne said in some distress.

"They may think they do, but as soon as they get used to having the road nearby they'll wonder how they ever managed without it."

"Do you think so?" she ventured, remembering that morning—how the Standard-bearer had led the throng of riders up the green hillside to a panorama of vales and streams and crags. "The longer I stay here, the more it seems to me they love and appreciate their own way of life. Perhaps it would be a pity to change it."

"But change is essential," Travers put in, "otherwise there can never be improvement."

"But *is* it improvement to bring a motorway here?" She hesitated. "Someone was telling me about some very interesting flowers on the hills here—"

"Oh, these blessed roses," Mr. Eldin broke in. "I know, I know. The rose thickets on the Burneybank are one of the most beautiful sights in the Borders when they're in bloom. But, my darling girl, who is going to suffer if we bulldoze them down?"

"You don't mean—You *can't* mean you've chosen a route along the Burneybank?" Corinne gasped.

"Look, this is no place to talk shop," Mr. Eldin said scoldingly. "After all, this is supposed to be a ball, not a business conference." He caught the eye of a passing waiter, to order champagne. Travers, taking the hint, asked Corinne if she would like to dance.

When they were out on the floor he said, "If you'd waited for me we could have come in together."

"But we hadn't made any arrangement, Trav—and I thought you might already be in the ballroom."

"I couldn't come until Dad was ready."

For one dreadful moment it was on the tip of her tongue to say, "Do you *have* to kow-tow to him like that?" But then she remembered the painful scenes that had sometimes occurred at the London office, and thought that it was only natural if Travers tried hard to keep his father in a good mood.

So she talked about something else. When the dance ended they went to join Norman Eldin at the table where he had settled, and found that Isabel Armstrong had already found him.

". . . Extraordinarily quiet," she was saying as they came up. "My editor's very disappointed."

"So sorry, my dear. I can't run my business just to please your editor." He laughed. "In any case, I've just been reprimanding Corinne for talking shop."

"Really?" Isa exclaimed, all alert. "What sort of shop were you talking?"

"Nothing in the least interesting, my dear. Besides which, a young lady in a party dress can surely be regarded as 'off duty'!"

"A reporter is never off duty," said Duncan, joining the group. "At least I assure you Isa never is."

"Good evening, Donaldson. Sit down, won't you? A very fine ball, I must say." He had to raise his voice to say this, for the dancers were now embarking on the Gay Gordons.

"So far it's been rather quiet," Isa observed.

"Quiet?"

"Oh yes, we've been known to make so much noise that they've heard us in Hawick."

"A slight exaggeration," Duncan put in, "but Isa's right—at the moment the noise level is lower than usual." He had taken a chair opposite Corinne, and now gave her a smile of congratulation. "You arrived just in time to see Corinne attempt her first eightsome reel, I think?"

Norman Eldin chuckled in good humour. "I rather rashly offered to partner her if there's another."

"Good for you. But I didn't see you at the Ride-out this morning?"

"No . . . er . . . I had some business to attend to."

"On a Saturday? What a pity."

Isa raised her eyebrows. "On a Saturday?" she repeated. "Must have been important!"

"As a matter of fact, it was."

"About the motorway?"

There was a momentary pause after this blunt question. Then Mr. Eldin said smoothly, "No, I've made no recommendation about the motorway."

Corinne was so taken aback at this outright lie that she couldn't prevent a quick intake of breath. Travers shot her a warning glance—but she had no intention of saying anything.

"I didn't ask you if you'd made any recommendation," Isa remarked in a thoughtful voice. "How interesting that you should mention the point . . ."

Mr. Eldin flushed, realizing he had made a blunder. "I think I did ask you not to talk shop," he said, raising his voice.

"Did you? I don't recall that. Were you in fact discussing the motorway today?"

"I haven't the slightest intention of discussing my business with you."

"Were you meeting with any officials of the Ministry of Highways?"

"Miss Armstrong . . . please . . ." Travers put in, looking apprehensive.

"*Were* you, Mr. Eldin?"

"No, I was not."

She considered that. "I don't think I believe you," she remarked.

"Isa," said Duncan, "don't make mischief."

"Why not? If you make mischief you make news. Who were you doing business with, Mr. Eldin?"

"My dear young woman, I haven't the slightest intention of telling you!"

She shrugged. "I'm pretty sure I can find out. You probably had a lunch with someone, because people aren't usually in their offices on a Saturday. So all I have to do is ring round the four-star hotels and restaurants. I think I'll go and do it now!"

"For goodness' sake, Isa," Duncan protested, "this is the Ride-out Ball! You can't walk out on it."

She turned on him with a rather hard smile. "I noticed *you* departed from tradition earlier today," she remarked. "The first time in fourteen years you haven't come home with the Standard-bearer..." She gave a momentary glint at Travers. "You weren't the only one waiting around at the Market Cross," she ended.

Duncan frowned at her. "So you waited, and I wasn't in the first three. That's no reason to take it out on other people. Do sit down and behave, Isa."

Slowly she resumed her seat. "You haven't even bothered to apologize," she muttered, but with some self-amusement in her voice now. "I don't know why I put up with you, Duncan Donaldson, I really don't!" She raised her straight brows at Corinne. "What on earth were you two doing up there for an hour and a half?"

"Talking about plants," Travers supplied.

"Plants?" Isa repeated.

Duncan turned a gaze of reproach on Corinne, who responded with a minute shake of the head to let him know she hadn't mentioned the rare orchid. She experienced a sudden lift of the spirits when he suddenly smiled.

He jumped up. "Would you care to dance?" he asked her.

Without stopping to think she rose too, and joined him on the dance floor.

"For one awful moment I thought you might have told Travers," he said.

"No, of course not. You said you'd only told the Botanical Society, so I guessed you wouldn't want it talked about."

"It's just that if people start tramping up there to look at it, they may damage it."

"Yes."

They danced in silence for a while.

"Enjoying the ball?" he enquired.

"Oh yes! It's so different from London!"

"No doubt." After a pause he said, "You're very quiet."

"Am I?"

"Was Travers very annoyed this afternoon?"

"Well . . . yes, he was."

"You didn't come back to the picnic."

"No." In fact she had collected her pony from the hitching rail and gone back with her to the riding stable.

"You really shouldn't allow other people to dominate you, Corinne."

"Do you think I do?"

"Well, don't you?"

Over the dark green cloth of his jacket she could see Travers watching them. The usual tremor of anxiety touched her. But after all, Trav and she were engaged.

Surely there was nothing wrong in wishing to please the man she was to marry?

Conversation dropped. She felt that if Trav continued to keep an eye on them, he could scarcely be displeased. They seemed to have nothing to say to each other. How strange, after the ease with which they had chatted that afternoon!

He took her back to the table and settled her there with a polite bow. "If you'll excuse me, I've some duty dances to attend to," he murmured.

Unconsciously she watched the tall figure in the braided jacket and dark tartan trousers make a path through the crowd. Who was he going to ask? Isa? No, Isa wouldn't be a duty dance. There was absolutely no reason to feel a twinge of envy when he paused to offer his hand to the schoolmaster's wife, a very attractive young woman in a romantically filmy dress.

Already the ball was going with a swing, but it mounted in gaiety and noise from there on. "What energy they've got," Mr. Eldin remarked as he led Corinne out for the next eightsome. "They've been leaping around for hours already." He gave her a kindly smile. "It's all right for a little girl like you, but if I get through this whole set I'll be jolly surprised. You won't mind if we fall out halfway?"

She was about to protest that that wouldn't be fair to the others in the reel, but a glance around her showed one or two couples who had been unable to fit into an eight, standing around the perimeter and tapping their feet to the music.

In fact, Mr. Eldin got through to the end, though he was mopping his face with his handkerchief at the last few bars. But the dancers, by now fully wound up, stamped and cheered and demanded an encore. The accordionist immediately led the band into another chord, men and women bowed and curtseyed, and it was clear they were off again.

"Oh *no*," groaned Norman Eldin. "Come along, my dear . . ."

"May I?" said a voice—and it was Duncan.

"Ah, right you are," Mr. Eldin said, about to give up his place at once.

"My turn now, I think," said Travers, appearing from his other side.

"Sorry," Duncan said, laughing, "but I got here first."

Travers turned with a confident smile to Corinne. He held out his hand and she took it, just in time to be whisked off in the first circling movement. And though she looked back to see how Duncan took it, she couldn't see him—he had mingled with the groups watching the reel.

One thing Corinne soon learned about old-fashioned country dancing—you meet a lot of men! The continual changing of partners in the reels, the Lancers, and something mysteriously known as the Circassian Circle, brought her into contact with one new face after another. In the modern dances these men would appear, inviting her to take the floor. She was on her feet almost from the moment she arrived until, all of a sudden at midnight, the band finished a tune and then played a long chord.

"What's happening?" she asked her current partner.

"Time for Auld Lang Syne."

"But it's only just twelve o'clock!"

"Oh, aye, but in a minute's time it'll be the Sabbath." Seeing her bewilderment he added, "I know it's different in big cities, Corinne, like you're used to, but hereabouts nobody dances or drinks on a Sunday. And in precisely—" he glanced at his watch—"two minutes, ten seconds, it'll be Sunday. So we stop now."

And so they did. Everyone joined hands in an enormous circle, the band played, and everybody sang. What was more, they all knew the words. Instead of repeating the first verse, which in Corinne's experience was all everybody ever did, this crowd sang :

> "And here's a hand, my trusty fiere,
> And gies a hand o' thine;
> We'll meet again some ither nicht
> For auld lang syne."

"Good gracious, what did all that mean?" she asked as the circle broke up to the soft playing of another tune.

"It's a slight adaptation of a poem by Robert Burns. It means, 'Here's a hand, my good friend, give me yours in exchange, we'll meet again another night for the sake of the good old days.' "

"Really? I'd no idea there were other verses, or that it was actually written by anybody. I thought it was just . . . you know . . . a folk song." She paused. "What's that he's playing now?"

"That's our 'goodbye' tune—'Haste Ye Back'." With a smile and a bow he left her to join his home-going family.

Corinne stood a moment, thinking how close and warm the relationships were in this community. 'Haste Ye Back' . . . She couldn't recall a single party that she had ever been to where there was a special tune that meant 'goodbye'.

Travers came to her side. "That was sudden, wasn't it?" he remarked with amusement. "They're an odd lot . . ."

"I was just thinking that it's rather charming."

"Oh? Well, everyone to their own taste. What happens now?"

It was clear that the party was dividing up into groups to go to each other's houses and continue on a private basis. Corinne saw one or two people glance her way, but since she was with Travers and was now joined by his father, no one seemed to think fit to invite her. She heard car doors slamming outside, people calling: "See you at Hamilton's in fifteen minutes" or "Are you for Lennox? Give me a lift then."

She wished someone would ask her to go. It would be fun to go to the Hamiltons' big kitchen at this hour of the night and perhaps talk and laugh till daybreak.

But Mr. Eldin said, "Look, my boy, it's rather lucky we've broken up so early. I want you to go out with me first thing in the morning to check that route inch by inch. Sir James is coming to look at it on Monday."

Travers frowned. "Oh, Dad, the night's young—"

"But *I* am not! I want to have a chat with you and then to bed."

"But Corinne—?"

"What about Corinne?" The older man turned to her with some impatience, pulling at his military moustache. "You've got your car, haven't you?"

"Yes, Mr. Eldin."

"Good. Then goodnight, my dear. Come along, Trav."

Travers hesitated. For one awful moment she thought he was going to follow his father like a sheep.

But he said, "I'll see Corinne out to her car, Dad."

"Oh?" It seemed he hesitated over saying "Come this minute." But instead he nodded. "Don't be long, then. I'll see you in my room."

To Corinne there was a strange upside-down feeling

about the situation. Normally the man sees the girl to her home, but here the positions were reversed : Trav *was* home, and it was Corinne who had to say goodnight and go.

Hers was the only car left in the car park. Trav's arm was about her as they walked to it.

"It's chilly now," he said. "Got a coat, darling?"

"In the car."

"Did you enjoy the ball?"

"It was great fun."

"A bit noisy. My head's splitting." He sighed. "And now Dad wants a business conference."

"Oh, what a shame, Trav. It's come on suddenly, hasn't it?" For a moment ago he had seemed ready to continue the party elsewhere.

"I suppose it's the thought of checking the route tomorrow. And Sir James on Monday."

"Yes, I can see it's a big thing. Who's Sir James?"

"Sir James Prudholme, adviser to the Ministry. He'll say yes or no to the route for the motorway."

"Gracious, he's important, then."

"He certainly is . . . But let's not talk about him. Let's talk about us. I wanted to take you into Edinburgh on Monday to choose a ring, but that's out now because of Sir James. We'll go Tuesday."

"No, we can't," she reminded him. "There's a Mr. Elphinstone from Carlisle, remember? He's bringing the plans for his factory."

"Confound it! I'd forgotten. Wednesday?"

"I think Wednesday would be all right."

"Splendid!"

He was taking her in his arms to kiss her when a window on the first floor lit up, bathing them in its reflection. Corinne stiffened in embarrassment : she knew instinctively that that was Norman Eldin's room, and that he had pulled back the curtains to see if she had gone yet.

"Oh, lord," muttered Travers.

"You'd better go. Goodnight, Trav."

"Oh, Corinne, listen—"

"I'll see you on Monday. You'll be busy tomorrow."

"Wait a minute, darling—"

The window on the first floor was pushed up. "Travers! Are you going to be long?"

Corinne busied herself with unlocking the car door. "Goodnight, Trav."

"Oh, all *right*!" he said savagely, and turning, walked indoors.

She sat for a long moment at the wheel, wondering why she had behaved like that. She had wanted to force Trav to make a stand, for once—was that it? If, eventually, they were going to announce their plans to Mr. Eldin, wasn't it necessary to prepare him in advance? And kissing his girl goodnight was surely a good demonstration of a growing seriousness in their relationship. Trav should have stood his ground...

She sighed and turned on the ignition. But though she pressed the starter again and again, the engine wouldn't catch. The starter engine whined and died each time: the motor wouldn't turn over.

"Botheration," she muttered to herself. What was she supposed to do next? She switched off for a moment, then searched in the glove compartment for the book of instructions. Not that they would be much help if it was something serious—she scarcely knew one thing from another in a car engine.

The booklet recommended that she should wait and

try again. This she did, with the same result. Now she was supposed to check the battery . . .

"Can I help you?"

She glanced out. Duncan was leaning down at the window.

"Oh . . . Duncan . . . What are you doing here? I thought you'd have gone with one of the groups."

"I'm just on my way, as a matter of fact—but I heard your starter wheezing. Anything I can do?"

"Well, thank you . . . do you know what might be wrong?"

"Let me have a look. Release the bonnet, will you?" She did so. He lifted it and his head disappeared from view. "Try it so I can see . . ."

For about ten minutes she obeyed his various instructions. "Got it," he said. "It's the low tension—it's loose at one of the attachment points."

"But how can that have happened, Duncan?"

"Oh, jolting over that track to your cottage. Just a minute, I'll try winding the ends . . ."

This time the starter turned and so did the engine. "There you are," he said, "but you'd better be careful how you take the road because it could shake loose—it really needs soldering."

"You mean I could come to a stop on the road over the moor?" she asked, alarmed.

"I'm afraid you could. But all you have to do is—" He broke off. "Look, I'll come with you, shall I? Then if it happens again I can put it right."

"Would you? Oh, thank you! I'd be so grateful." Then she thought again. "But what about you? You were on your way somewhere."

"To the Lennoxes'. It's okay—I can walk from your cottage to their farm."

"But it's over a mile!"

He laughed. "You say that as if it's the journey of the century. That's only a quarter of an hour's walk—and you know I'm accustomed to being out on the moor at night."

"I don't really think I—"

"You must allow me," he said firmly, opening the passenger door and getting in. "I couldn't be easy if you drove off alone. I enjoy the moors at night, but I don't think *you* would."

"N-no . . . Very well, thank you, Duncan."

Corinne drove away from the hotel with care. Duncan asked if she had enjoyed the ball; she said she had. Then he said, "Why are you going home so early?"

"No one invited us to go to one of the get-togethers." As she said it she realized she sounded wistful.

"I suppose everyone assumed that you and Travers . . ."

"He and his father have to have a quick discussion."

"Tonight? Couldn't it wait till tomorrow?"

"Oh, no, because tomorrow they have to go out and check—"

"Check what?"

"Nothing," she replied, realizing she had better be careful.

"Ah," he said. She was busy watching the road, but she could tell he was smiling in ironic amusement. She guessed he knew very well that tomorrow's "check" had something to do with the new motorway.

She had a mental picture of his face that afternoon as he parted the coarse grass that protected the orchid.

"Duncan," she said.

"Yes?"

"I don't want to be disloyal to Trav."

"Of course not."

"I just want you to know that . . . well . . . I'm awfully sorry."

"About what?"

She moved uncomfortably. "About . . . what's going to happen. I think it's going to make you very unhappy."

He was silent.

"I'd like to say that . . . well, I'm not happy about it either."

"You mean that they're going to hack up my countryside and you wish they weren't?"

"Yes."

"Then why don't you do something about it?"

"Such as what?"

"Help us! Tell us what's hanging over us!"

"But you *know* that, Duncan. There's a motorway—"

"But which route is it going to take? And when are they going to start on it?" Suddenly he laid a hand on her arm, his fingers warm on the bare flesh. "We need your help, Corinne!"

She felt suddenly very strange—weak and lost. So much so that for a moment the car veered wildly on the empty road. Duncan snatched away his hand to steady the wheel. The moment his touch left her arm, it was as if a current were switched off and she was herself again.

"I'm very sorry," she said, almost briskly. "It's not my place to take a hand in such matters."

"Not your place? How can you talk like that! You're a human being with a right to your own opinions! If you think the motorway is wrong—"

"I didn't say that," she broke in. "I don't know

whether it's right or wrong, because I haven't enough knowledge of these things."

"But *we* think it's wrong. We don't want it, Corinne!"

"You're only speaking for yourself, surely."

"Not a bit of it. Do you really think I've done nothing in the months since we first got wind of this scheme? I can bring a thousand people to any meeting they may hold about planning permission! The farmers are against it because it'll wreck the sheep pastures, the anglers are against it because it almost certainly means damage to the fishing, the villagers are against it because it means a dangerous and noisy road—"

She was staggered. "I'd no idea you'd got that far. You didn't mention any of this."

"To you?" he said, with a faint bitterness. "Do you really think we'd give away our plans to the enemy?"

"The enemy . . ." The word hung between them.

"I'm sorry," he said. "I didn't really mean that." With a gentle finger he put back a thick lock of hair that was screening her face from him, and once again she felt that glow under his touch. "I think you want to be a friend," he murmured.

"Oh yes. Yes, I do!"

"Then help us, please, Corinne. Your boss Norman Eldin has a big business behind him, and the support of the Ministry of Highways—"

"Oh!" she gasped.

"What? What, Corinne?"

"There's an official coming on Monday—"

"Where? Here? To Burney?"

But once again she made herself stop. All her instincts were shouting at her to pour it all out, to help Duncan and the other friends she had made here in

Burney—but her training as a secretary was like a stone wall preventing the flood of confession.

In a trembling voice she said, "I mustn't tell you, Duncan. I'm sorry, but as long as I'm working for Eldin Consultants my first loyalty lies with them."

"Then leave them."

"What?"

"Give up the job."

It was like a dash of cold water over her.

"Give up my job? But I can't. I couldn't do that."

"Nonsense, you could get a dozen jobs as good as that."

"No, no, you don't understand. I don't *want* to."

For a moment she thought he was going to continue the argument. A moment later her cottage came into sight, shining in the light of a young moon in a starry sky.

She drew up on the sandy gravelly patch by her door. "Would you like to come in for a drink or anything?" she invited.

He shook his head as he got out. "No, thank you. The others will be wondering where I've got to." He pushed the car door closed, then came round to help her out.

"Corinne," he said, urgency in his voice, "you could be an enormous help to us in our campaign. Please give up your job and come over to our side. You could tell us a thousand things we need to know."

She drew away from him. "You couldn't really ask me to do that. I'd feel a . . . a traitor!"

"To what? To the firm, or to Travers Eldin?"

"To both."

"Oh, how can you waste your time—!" He stopped speaking abruptly, then seized her by the shoulders and shook her with an anger that he could no longer contain. "How can you waste your time on a man like that?"

Her breath was taken away. She could make no reply. They stared at each other in the pale light. His hands were still on her shoulders, grasping her cruelly.

"You may like to know," she said in a voice scarcely above a whisper, "that Travers and I got engaged this afternoon."

There was a sudden blaze in his eyes. His hands fell away.

"Oh well," he said with a shrug, "it doesn't matter. I've got the information I wanted from you anyhow."

Then he turned on his heel and walked away, his tall figure soon lost in the shadows of the moors.

CHAPTER SEVEN

AS if to reflect her mood, black clouds rolled up next day. Outside her cottage Corinne could see a drenched countryside. The stream at the foot of the slope began to brim up, and big puddles formed on the ground outside her door. The cottage windows were curtained in rainwater which ran in rivulets down the outside of the panes.

She worke late after sleeping badly; there had been long sessions of wakefulness between dream-haunted drowsings which finally gave way to an hour or two of deeper rest. She got up with some reluctance, knowing that today would not be a good day.

If the weather had been fine she would have gone for a long walk, or taken Minty out for a canter. But if she wanted to go anywhere today it would have to be by car—and the car needed attention.

About one o'clock she had a sandwich lunch, then decided to go up to Meg Moffat's farm and ask to use her telephone. She would get the man from the garage in Hawick to come out and either attend to the faulty connection at the cottage or drive it away to be mended at the workshop.

She was pretty confident that the little saloon would take her safely the short distance to the farm, and this proved correct. Meg herself opened the house door as she drew up. "Well, so there you are! Come away ben."

Corinne made a quick dash through the downpour to the safety of the house. "My, it's wet!"

"Aye, the burn will be overflowing soon, and maist like the Caith Water too. Well-a-well, never mind. Did ye enjoy the Ride-out Ball?"

"Ye—es."

Mrs. Moffat cocked her head. "You sound as if you ha'e your doots?"

"Never mind about that," Corinne said hurriedly. "I came to ask if I could use your phone, Mrs. Moffat? I'd like to ring the garage—"

"About your car? Och, that's all taken care of. Willie Stewart will be here about three o'clock to solder the loose connection."

"Mrs. Moffat!" Corinne cried. "How could you possibly arrange that, or even know about it?"

"It wasna me, my dear. It was Himself."

"He rang you?" Not for the first time she was quite overcome by a sense of bafflement. What kind of man was this, who one moment cruelly told her he had used her as a spy and the next went out of his way to do her a kindness?

127

"He was here himself, early. He's out with his binoculars and his map, you know."

Corinne stared at her. "No, I don't know. What do you mean?"

"Out watching them that's checking the motorway route. They're checking the layout, and he's checking *them*." The old lady gave a bright smile. "It has its comical side, has it no?"

"Not to me," Corinne thought. What would Travers say if he found out? *When* he found out? He would know that Duncan could have got the hint only from Corinne.

"Come, come, what's that sad face for? Even if the rain is coming down like a lyart linn, there's nae need to let it make you sad."

"Oh, it isn't that... Mrs. Moffat, is it true that Duncan's got a lot of supporters for a campaign against the motorway?"

"To be sure it is. Why should you doubt it?"

"But... but we've heard nothing of it."

"By 'we', you mean yourself and the Mister Eldins? Well, my dearie, why should we tell you, when it would be like handing you the rope with the whilk to hang us?"

Corinne gazed at her. "I really don't understand you. How can you say a thing like that, and yet be so nice to me?"

"Ah well, it's because you yourself are not really in your heart against us—now are you, lassie?"

"Oh, not if it means any harm to any of you—you *know* that, Mrs. Moffat. I only wish it had never been suggested to have a motorway!"

"And so say all of us! So you see, knowing that you feel like that, how could I be unkind?"

Mrs. Moffat began to busy herself making tea. Watching her, Corinne was struck by the feeling that Duncan was often here watching her like this.

"Did . . . did Duncan tell you anything else this morning?" she ventured.

"About the motorway? Aye, a thing or two." A cloud of steam enveloped her as she poured boiling water into the pot, so that Corinne couldn't see her face.

"Did he tell you about anything other than the motorway?"

"Ah," said Meg Moffat, dropping the lid on the brown pot with a little 'plop' of satisfaction, "some things he doesna need to *tell* me."

They were drinking the tea when, as foretold, a young man in a battered van arrived. He asked for Corinne's car keys, drove her car into one of Mrs. Moffat's barns, and returned twenty minutes later with the laconic information : "Yon's sorted."

"How much do I owe you?"

As soon as she had said it she knew it was a mistake. Willie Stewart looked offended, Mrs. Moffat looked surprised.

"A fine thing if I couldna do a favour for Himself without needing to be paid," Willie said.

"I'm sorry . . ."

"Oh, think nae mair o' it." He gave her a sudden bright grin, then looked hungrily at the fruit tart on the table. Seconds later he was contentedly gulping down a huge portion.

He escorted Corinne home later, giving her a cheery wave as he passed her and headed for Burney. Her answering wave was less cheery—one of the Eldin fieldwork vehicles was parked at her door. Her heart sank as she saw that Travers was sitting inside.

"Hello," she called. "Been here long?"

"About a quarter of an hour. Where have you been?"

"Up to the farm. Just a minute and I'll get the door open"

She darted from her car with the door key in her hand and almost immediately Travers followed her inside.

"Like some tea? I've just had some, but I'll make some for you."

"No, thanks."

"I thought you were to be out doing a final survey?"

"Yes, I'm rejoining them about four."

"How's it going?"

"Perfectly. Why shouldn't it?"

She studied him. The dark handsome eyes were stormy, his mouth was set. "What's the matter, Trav?"

"That's what I'm waiting to hear from *you*."

"From me?"

"I saw you last night!" he accused. "I looked out and saw you."

"And what," she enquired, feeling the beat of anger in her heart, "what did you see?"

"He got into your car with you, and you drove away!"

"Quite right."

"You don't deny it?"

"No."

"You brought him here in the middle of the night?"

"Yes."

"I'm waiting for your explanation."

"Sit down," she said, gesturing towards a chair. "You'll have a long wait."

They faced each other as adversaries, each cold with anger that was increased by fatigue and frustration.

Suddenly he took a step and engulfed her in his arms. "I'm sorry—darling, I'm sorry! Of course I know there's a simple explanation."

"There is," she gasped, vanquished by his action. "I don't know why I didn't just tell you when you asked."

"Because I'm a fool, that's why! Barging in here, accusing you of heaven knows what! I must be out of my mind. After all, we're *engaged*. You wouldn't look at another man—I know that."

"Of course not, darling—"

"I couldn't bear it if you did," he said. "I'd never forgive you, never, if you let me down."

"Trav, there's no need to have thoughts like that."

"No, I'm sure there isn't. I'm a fool. Forgive me?" He kissed her to seal the forgiveness.

At last he had to recall them both to everyday life. "I've got to get back to the team. It's a rotten day for a final survey. I hope it's not going to pour like this tomorrow when Sir James is here."

"I hope not, darling."

"Shall we have dinner somewhere special this evening? We ought to, as a celebration."

"Won't you be too tired after a day like this?"

"No, no—a bath and a change will make all the difference. I'll collect you about seven, shall I?"

"That will be fine."

As he reached the door he paused. "By the way, why *did* Donaldson drive away with you last night?"

When he had gone a sense of chill invaded her that, despite his protestations of trust, he had had to have the facts after all.

For the very first time, the thought formed in her mind: Are we right for one another?

It was a question she had never dreamed of asking

before. From the very first moment that she had seen Trav, she had been in love with him. He had been looking at applicants for the post of secretary, and as she came out of his office after the interview she was praying inwardly: "Please let him choose me. Please let him choose me."

Love at first sight. Was it just because he was so good to look at?

No, no, she protested to herself. There was so much else. At first their relationship had been strictly employer-employee, but he had been so kind, so appreciative of all her work. It was true he had demanded a lot, but he had noticed her efforts, and he had expressed his thanks. That meant such a lot. Corinne had worked for more than one boss who would have taken it entirely for granted if she had stayed at the office, typing all night.

But Trav wasn't like that. And when their relationship moved from office friendship to a more intimate plane, there had still been that warmth and responsiveness. He had always *prized* her—that was the word. It was as if he saw her as something, some*one*, very special, who would make his life more complete. Someone on whom he had to reiterate his claims, in case she turned away?

Some lines of poetry came into her mind.

"Farewell! thou art too dear for my possessing..."

How did it go on? Something about

"And for that riches where is my deserving?"

There was something of that feeling in Trav's outlook. Perhaps it was to do with his father's domination of him; it had given him a feeling that he wasn't quite good enough—not good enough as an engineer or a businessman, nor as a man in everyday life...

No, no, she mustn't think such things! What had come over her that she should sit here analysing Trav dispassionately, almost callously?

It was because Duncan had said: "How can you waste time on a man like that!"

Now here she was, wondering, a man like what? What was Trav like, really? Did she know?

In their London setting she had been sure she knew all about him. They went everywhere together, shared the same interests. It was because they had moved out of that setting that everything had changed. Now their tastes were diverging—or at least Corinne's were.

That was the trouble, wasn't it? *She* was changing. She was developing new interests, new attitudes. The friction between herself and Trav was caused by the fact that she was changing and he was not.

So it was all her fault. If, in the last few days, she and Trav were in a state of collision, it was because she was continually upsetting his accepted view of her. She must call a halt. It was only fair to Trav that she should remain as she had been before, that she should retrace the steps that had taken her away from him to even a slight extent. She must banish from her mind the strange uneasiness roused by Duncan.

Why, why, *why* should she distress herself over something he had said? He was nothing to her, absolutely nothing. All he ever did was manoeuvre her into making unguarded remarks, manipulate her so that she was 'useful' to him. How could she be so absurdly vulnerable as to worry about anything put into her mind by a man like that?

Nevertheless it clouded her evening with Trav. Only when they were saying goodnight, and she was able to abandon herself to his kisses, could she drown out that little echo of doubt.

Next day Sir James Prudholme arrived at the Eldin Consultants office in Hawick. He proved to be a stocky, weathered, ugly man with silver hair and a voice like emery paper—a real toughie, Corinne said to herself.

He spent an hour looking at the reports on the soil samples and the contour maps He talked about the geology of the area. He shuffled the sheets of plans and estimates as if they were playing cards in his big hands. He said little, although he seemed pleased.

Corinne had been instructed to book a table for lunch for all of them at the Burney House Hotel. She was to attend, to take notes if need be. Immediately after lunch Sir James was to be driven to the approximate route of the new road so that he could see for himself in living detail the difficulties or assets of the chosen levels.

All four of them got into Trav's big Citroën—Corinne's car was left at the office, for she would be returning there at some time of the day to type up her notes. During the drive out to the village of Burney, Sir James began to seem a little more amiable.

"My Minister would like this business settled before the end of the year," he said to Norman Eldin, "so that we can get the Bill for construction of the motorway through Parliament in the spring. There won't be any hold-ups, I take it?"

"None at all," Norman assured him.

Corinne, sitting beside Trav in the front, made a stifled sound.

"Did you say something, m'dear?"

"N—no, Sir James. I just wondered . . ."

"Eh? What? What?"

"Whether there might be some opposition."

"Ah," said Sir James, "I've heard a thing or two. I keep my ear to the ground, y'know. Did you know, Eldin, that there was a reporter from the local paper checking up on us?"

"No!" gasped Mr. Eldin in alarm.

"Uh-huh. There was. Still, what good would it do, even if they found out now about our meetings?"

"None at all, so far as I can see."

"More worrying to me, as a matter of fact, is this hint I've had that Lord Caithdale isn't in favour of the scheme."

"Oh, I don't place much weight on that," Mr. Eldin replied, relaxing. "He hasn't bothered to *do* anything, has he? And besides, I've checked the land titles—he doesn't own anything around there. He sold out years ago. So what difference does it make if he's in favour or not?"

"I don't know," said the Ministry official, with some doubt in his voice. "These old land-owners often have a lot of influence."

"But he hasn't bothered to show up—"

"Perhaps that's because so far there's been no definite plan," Corinne put in. "Once the announcement of the route is made . . ."

"Ah, you think he might turn up then, m'dear? Well, let him. He won't be much of a rallying-point if he's so late on the scene as all that."

"I quite agree with you, Sir James," Trav said over his shoulder. "There was a spot of bother at the beginning, as you may recall. But I feel sure everything will be plain sailing from now on."

The first indication that he was completely wrong came when he swung the big car round the last bend of the country road and into the drive of the hotel. There were two big vans parked there: one bore the lettering "BBC" and the other "Border Television".

"Oh, help," Corinne said under her breath.

It took a moment longer for the implication to sink in on the others. Trav slowed almost to a standstill.

"Television coverage?" he exclaimed. "Who for?"

Sir James made an angry sound. "For us, you numbskull! Who else?"

"Perhaps there's a visiting celebrity—here for the fishing—"

"Nonsense!"

By this time the car had crept to the hotel entrance. It was clear to the evidence of their own eyes that the television cameras set up on either side were trained on the car's occupants.

As Trav put on the brakes, a big group of people suddenly emerged from the shrubbery at the side of the hotel. It was beautifully timed. Just as Sir James Prudholme and Mr. Eldin got out, a little forest of placards sprang up.

"Hands Off Our Hills!" one protested. Another read, "No Bulldozers at Burney!" and a third "Motorway Madness!"

The crowd surrounded them as they moved towards the hotel doorway. A splendidly disciplined chant arose: "Out! Out! Prudholme out!"

"Good heavens!" growled Sir James. "They've even got my name!"

"You've wasted your journey!

We don't want you at Burney!" chanted the crowd.

They were all perfectly good-humoured, but there were at least thirty of them and their very number was intimidating. Corinne clung to Trav's arm and, in the midst of a tight group made by the men, was hurried into the hotel, head down and shoulders hunched as if in self-protection.

"My hat!" panted Sir James as they reached the safety of the vestibule. "That was a surprise."

Poor Mr. Eldin was beside himself. "I can only apologize, Sir James—"

"Nonsense, man, it isn't your fault."

Mr. Patterson, the owner of the hotel, came forward to usher them to their table. There were one or two tables already occupied, and it was with a lurch of her heart that Corinne saw Duncan and Isa together at the far side of the dining-room.

"What are they doing there?" she said in a low voice to Mr. Patterson.

He raised his eyebrows. "Having lunch," he said innocently.

She understood at once that Patterson was an ally of the protesters. After all, why shouldn't he be? The proposed motorway would shatter the peace of his hotel, carve up the hillside so that his view was wrecked, and spoil the fishing for the anglers who made up a large part of his clientele.

They settled in their places. The waitress came with the menus, and the wine waiter to take orders for drinks. Nothing more occurred until the little lull that ensued afterwards.

Then, to Corinne's dismay, Duncan rose from his place, to walk across the restaurant.

"Sir James, may I speak to you on behalf of the Burneybank Protest Group?"

"Who the devil are you?" Sir James said, glaring up at him.

"This is Duncan Donaldson, a local resident," Travers said, rather pale with apprehension.

"Uh-*huh*," said Sir James. "Well, why are you here, young man? Can't you let a chap have his lunch in peace?"

"This is more important than your lunch, sir. The residents of the village of Burney and the dwellers in Caithdale wish to protest most strongly at the proposal to spoil our countryside—"

"You're taking a great deal upon yourself, my dear sir," interrupted Sir James. "How can you possibly know that your countryside is going to be spoiled?"

"We know that there's a plan for a motorway, and we know the route. The members of the Protest Group—"

"You cannot possibly know the route! It hasn't been published!"

"We know it," Duncan insisted. "I followed the survey team step by step yesterday as they made their final check."

There followed a stunned silence. Corinne could feel her colour rising at the thought that this was all her fault. She dared not look up, but she was sure that Trav was staring accusingly at her.

Sir James blew out an angry breath. "Well, go on, say what you have to say," he growled.

"The people of Caithdale don't want a motorway. Its construction would pollute the Caith Water and destroy the burnet roses on the Burneybank which have been there for generations. It would swallow up large sections of grazing for our sheep. It would damage our environment. We refuse to allow it to be constructed, and we want you to know this *now*, before you embark on any further development."

The calm authority of his tone was such that Corinne raised her head to look at him as he spoke. The tall angular figure seemed to dominate the room. All the other clients of the hotel had turned in their places to watch what was going on. Isa was just behind him with her notebook in her hand, her deep-set eyes alight with an almost malicious interest. In the kitchen doorway, Nell the waitress and one or two members of the staff were looking on approvingly.

Sir James said in a cool tone: "I am glad to have your views. However, it would be more appropriate to wait for the public announcement of the scheme and the subsequent inquiry."

"I'm sorry, but past experience has shown that once a scheme gets to the stage of a public inquiry it's often too late to prevent it. We want you to know *now* that we utterly reject the idea of a motorway across the Burneybank."

"I will report your remarks to my Minister. But I think you must accept that this road is coming. I'm here today to examine the route."

"If you were to report against it, the idea would be dropped."

Sir James frowned. "I have nothing more to say," he remarked, with a glance at Isa's busy hand skimming over her notebook.

Duncan met his frowning gaze. "Very well," he said. "You can expect more opposition."

"Good afternoon, young man. I'd like to get on with my lunch if you don't mind."

Duncan gave a little bow and withdrew. The atmosphere relaxed, the wine waiter came with the sherry.

"Phew!" said Mr. Eldin. "That was a surprise."

"They're a smart bunch," Sir James muttered. "Who did you say that was, the spokesman?"

"Duncan Donaldson. He sells tractors and so forth."

"Umm. And the girl?"

"She . . . she was probably the reporter you mentioned as checking up on us. She got on the track at the ball held here on Saturday night. She must have spent all day yesterday checking up on the restaurants and hotels." Norman Eldin tugged angrily at his moustache. "But I can't understand how they found out about the final survey yesterday."

Corinne was opening her mouth to confess when Sir James swept on: "It doesn't matter how. What's important is how many people share the view that chap has just put forward. Is he just a crank, or what?"

"He's no crank," Corinne said.

"You know him, do you? What's he like?"

"He's a crank," Trav put in before she could reply. "He's one of those types who get worked up about plants and trees. Quite absurd, really. Everybody knows that the surroundings have got to be carved up a bit when road-making goes on."

"I wouldn't discount him on that account," Sir James said. "People get very worked up about the environment these days, and we've got to be prepared for opposition. For instance, is Lord Caithdale involved with this bunch?"

They all looked gloomy, and the lunch progressed in an atmosphere of unease. Nell served them with a cold efficiency quite at variance with her usual friendly manner. Corinne had her shorthand notebook ready, but the men felt unable to discuss construction details for fear anything was overheard by the supporters of the protest.

When the meal was over they had to nerve themselves to go out. They knew, from the murmur of voices outside, that the protesters hadn't gone away. As they came out of the entrance, the TV cameramen focused on them, the placards and the banners were hoisted, and the chanting recommenced.

This time Corinne saw Duncan in the forefront. He looked in complete control of the situation.

"Come on," Mr. Eldin said anxiously. "Trav, get the car ready—engine running and all that."

Trav pushed his way through the protesters, who did nothing to stop him. He opened the door of the Citroën, got in, unlocked the other doors so that the passengers could get in quickly.

As he started the engine, Duncan called, *"Now!"*

A little group of six people separated themselves from the main crowd. Among them Corinne recognized two of the men she had met at the ball, the postmistress, and Meg Moffat. Meg's wrinkled face was set in lines of utter determination. She clutched a pole to which was attached a card : "Sheep Must Safely Graze!"

To Corinne's consternation these six people, with Duncan at their head, took up a position about three feet from the Citroën's front fender.

They were so close to the car that if Trav moved forward they would either have to scatter or be hit by the bonnet. He sat with his hands on the wheel, staring at them uncertainly through the windscreen.

"Drive forward!" called his father. "Go on, Trav!"

At that moment Mrs. Moffat began to sing in a voice of quavering sweetness. But not one of the usual protest songs—not "We Shall Not Be Moved", or "We Shall Overcome". The words floated in the sudden stillness.

> "I to the hills will lift mine eyes,
> From whence doth come mine aid.
> My safety cometh from the Lord
> Who Heaven and Earth hath made."

Instantly the entire crowd of protesters joined in:

> "My foot He'll not let slide, nor will
> He slumber that me keeps . . ."

It was clear they all knew it well. Their voices rang out, strong and full.

"What on earth is *that*?" grumbled Sir James.

"It . . . it sounds like a psalm," Corinne ventured, "but a bit different."

"A psalm?"

"From the Bible."

"It's Psalm one hundred and twenty-one," said Nell the waitress in a tone that implied 'Everyone knows that!' "It's the metrical version we use in Scottish churches."

"Uh-*huh*," said Sir James, with an irate glance at the television crews. "They're just lapping it up!"

"Drive on, Trav!" shouted Mr. Eldin.

The Citroën inched foward.

And all the protesters in front of it, as if at a signal, sat down.

There was no doubt it had all been planned with minute care. Each step had been calculated for maximum propaganda effect. Trav, scared almost out of his wits, stopped dead—only inches away from Mrs. Moffat's shoulder.

The old lady threw back her head, to stare defiantly around. Her snapping black eyes met Corinne's. Corinne was horrified.

"Meg!" she cried. "Meg, get up!"

It had poured in torrents yesterday, and even today there had been intermittent showers from a grey-flecked sky. The gravel drive of the hotel was sodden. It was not a suitable place for anyone to sit down, let alone an eighty-year-old lady.

Without stopping to think what she was doing, Corinne turned away from the car door and rushed to Mrs. Moffat's side, right in amongst the sit-down.

"Mrs. Moffat!" she pleaded. "Meg! Get up, you'll catch your death of cold!"

The old lady smiled up at her. "My dear lassie," she murmured, and held up her hand.

Corinne took it, expecting to help her to her feet. Instead Mrs. Moffat pulled hard, and Corinne subsided among the seated protesters.

"Welcome!" cried the postmistress, and seized her other hand.

Trapped and helpless, Corinne struggled to get up again. But while she was still doing so Trav slammed his car into reverse, his father and Sir James clambered in, and they were away.

After that Corinne wasn't quite sure of the sequence of events. She remembered helping Mrs. Moffat to her feet and trying to dust wet gravel from her black coat. She remembered a young man thrusting a microphone into her face, but what he asked and what she replied she couldn't recall. There was some laughter and more singing. Then they all crowded into the lounge of the hotel for coffee and sandwiches, including the television reporters who seemed to be enjoying themselves enormously. They particularly singled out Meg Moffat.

And Meg was a natural-born television personality. "They'll no build a road across my property," she declared, "even if I have to camp out all day and all night to prevent them. Besides which, it's a daft idea."

"How do you mean, daft?"

"The ground isna suitable. I've lived eighty years

143

and more in these hills, and I can tell you, the place is honeycombed with caves and such. When I'm dowsing for water, oft I feel the emptiness—"

"You're a dowser? Have you had much success?"

The reporters turned the talk to her prowess as a water-diviner. Corinne felt they must have used up miles of recording tape on Mr. Moffat, but later when they had moved elsewhere she said to her: "Is that right, about the caves?"

"It surely is. The old Border reivers used them to hide stolen cattle or for shelter against attacks."

"Like the one that's supposed to be near Catherine's Tower?"

"Aye, exactly like. The passage to that one has fallen in, but mind me, there's many others we've no memory of. Only the hazel twig has told me they're there, and if they start cutting up the surface for a motorway they'll like as not fall through!"

"But surely ... the surveyors can tell if the surface is thin?"

"How? They don't go deep enough when they take their wee samples of soil and rock. Below that shell of soil, there's hollowness."

"Would you tell all that to Mr. Eldin?"

"Oh, he'll no listen to *me*. You tell him, Corinne."

"He's not going to listen to me either, after that terrible trick you played on me, Mrs. Moffat."

"It wasn't so terrible. You belonged with us in spirit, surely. You don't want to see the Burneybank scarred by a great ugly motorway, do you?"

"No, but I didn't want to join a sit-down about it either!" Corinne sighed. "I ought to be very angry with you. Did ... did Duncan tell you to do what you did?"

"Duncan? How could he know you were going to hurry to my side? Besides," Mrs. Moffat said with a determined tilt of her chin, "I dinna need a man to tell me what to do!"

"No," thought Corinne in envy, "she's a complete, independent personality in her own right . . ."

About four o'clock the television crews packed up and left, the protesters began to disperse homewards. Duncan had vanished from the scene early on, along with Isa Armstrong.

"Well now, I'm for home," Mrs. Moffat said. "And you, my dearie?"

"I've got to go back to the office—I don't know whether Mr. Eldin or Travers will be back yet, but they may have dictation for me. That is," she added, "if they don't fire me on the spot."

"Och, they wouldn't be so unjust, to be angry with you because of a prank of mine!" The old lady patted her hand. "Besides, even if Mr. Eldin was in a temper, your young man would stand up for you, would he no?"

Corinne was by no means sure. "Anyhow, I've got to go and face the music, and collect my car."

"I'll give you a lift into town then. Come on, lassie."

When Corinne went into the office she expected to be summoned at once to account for her actions. But the junior told her that the Eldins had not come back yet, and though she waited until long after the usual time of finishing they didn't come. At length she locked up and went home. And there, sitting in front of her portable television set with a meal on a tray, she discovered why the Eldins had not come back to the office.

The news magazine programme was making much of

the proposed motorway. There were interviews with one or two prominent people. Then the announcer explained that the inhabitants of Caithdale had staged a protest that afternoon. Shots followed, illustrating the sit-down, and then personality profiles of those taking part. Meg Moffat came across full of life and determination.

Then to Corinne's utter dismay, there she was herself, looking confused and upset.

"You work for the firm of engineering consultants, I believe?" the reporter asked.

"Yes."

"Yet you decided to take part in this protest?"

"No, that was an accident."

"But you do think the scheme for the motorway is wrong?"

"I don't really know. When they sang that thing about the hills... After all, they are *their* hills..."

"Exactly," said the announcer in the studio. "And here they are among their hills."

Next came film taken, obviously, immediately afterwards—there had been cameramen waiting on the route taken by Trav's car. And now Corinne understood where Duncan had got to.

There he was among a group of horsemen, led by the young Standard-bearer of Saturday's celebrations. They rode to and fro in front of the car, causing it to jerk to a stop at every yard or so. At one or two points, where the surveyors had set up markers, they made a sort of equestrian maypole-dance with them.

Once again it was superb propaganda. There was something chivalrous about them, mounted on their sturdy hill ponies, led by the boy with the flag, making

146

circles round the streamlined car which was really quite unsuitable for the unsurfaced roads on the slopes.

While the film was shown the commentator explained that this was the route the motorway was supposed to take. "The Burneybank, one of the most beautiful hills in the Border Country..." "The little unspoilt village of Burney..." "Much damage expected to the trout-fishing..." "Sheep country ruined..."

Back to the studio. The announcer finished cheerfully: "Thanks to the Border raiders in action in our film, the engineers and the representative from the Ministry of Highways were unable to finish their survey. In fact, we understood their car broke down about halfway..."

Corinne switched it off. She dreaded to think what Mr. Eldin had said in the face of this débâcle. To be stopped in his tracks like this—to be made a fool of, in public!—oh, he would have been furious!

Tomorrow she would have to face his rage. She trembled at the thought. And then, all at once, she felt a sudden surge of courage. If an old lady like Meg Moffat could take part in a public protest and carry a banner, surely she—Corinne Lenwood, about a quarter her age—could stand up to Norman Eldin.

In fact, she would take the wind out of his sails. She would hand in her resignation!

Next day, bright and early, she drove to the office. She typed out a letter ready to hand to Mr. Eldin, explaining that she felt it was best to part company. When the office junior arrived at nine Corinne had already opened the post and started the day's work. She wanted no grounds for complaint against her efficiency in the office.

Norman Eldin came in alone. He nodded at Corinne

as he went through the outer office. "I want to speak to you at once."

Picking up her letter of resignation, she followed him. He was taking off his raincoat as she entered his room—it had been raining since dawn.

"Confounded weather!" he grumbled. "Sit down, Corinne."

"I'd rather stand."

"What? Oh, please yourself. Well, yesterday was a fiasco, wasn't it!"

"Yes, and I'm sorry, Mr. Eldin. I realize how it must look to you, and so I want to—"

"You've got friends among that crowd, obviously."

"I'm afraid that's true. I've grown very fond of some of the people, particularly Mrs. Moffat and—"

"You could do us a lot of good, you know."

Corinne stared. "*I* could?"

"Particularly with Lord Caithdale. He's the brains behind it all, obviously."

"Lord Caithdale? But I don't know Lord Caithdale."

Norman Eldin smiled rather fiercely. "Oh yes, you do, my dear. Duncan Lewis Fernand Donaldson, seventh Earl of Caithdale."

The room seemed to swim in front of Corinne's eyes.

"Duncan?" she breathed.

" 'Himself'," Mr. Eldin said. "And the gossip is that he rather likes you."

CHAPTER EIGHT

CORINNE needed some moments to recover from the shock. Mr. Eldin was still talking, but she didn't take in a word he was saying.

Duncan was Lord Caithdale. She tried to grasp the fact and all its implications. Lord Caithdale had been mentioned now and again since she got mixed up in the affairs of Burney and its inhabitants—but just at this moment she couldn't recall what had been said about him.

But now, of course, she understood why the local people referred to Duncan as "Himself". In a way it had always intrigued her, this instinctive respect they seemed to accord him—but now it was explained. His family had been important in the locality—probably had been landowners, leaders, decision-makers.

She suddenly broke into Norman Eldin's monologue. "What makes you imagine I could have any influence with . . . with Lord Caithdale?"

He broke off, surprised. Then, recovering, he said, "Travers tells me—"

"Travers somehow got hold of quite the wrong idea. I assure you, Mr. Eldin, Duncan Donaldson has a very poor opinion of me."

"I think you're mistaken," he objected, shaking his head. "From the very outset he put himself out on your behalf. I don't know if you recall it, but I was rather angry when you first let slip the information about the motorway. Well, we got a roundabout hint that Lord Caithdale felt you shouldn't be victimized over that."

Corinne blushed. "But that was probably just his sense of fair play! I mean, since Lord Caithdale and

Duncan Donaldson are one and the same person, and it was to Duncan that I blurted out the information, he probably felt he owed me that much."

"Travers tells me that on Saturday—"

"Oh, for goodness' sake!" she burst out, uncaring that she was interrupting her employer quite rudely. "Just because Duncan and I walked back into the village from the Ride-out...! I *explained* all that to Trav. And anyhow, since then..."

"Since then, what?"

"We ... we had a row."

"You and Trav?"

"No—with Duncan. On Saturday night. Sunday morning, rather."

"When the ball ended? But you went home."

"Duncan went with me."

Mr. Eldin raised his brows. "That doesn't seem like indifference to me."

She tried to collect her thoughts so as to explain to him how it had all come about. She was still seeking for words when the door of Mr. Eldin's office was flung open and the junior came in, with Isa Armstrong on her heels.

"I'm sorry, Mr. Eldin, she wouldn't take no for an answer—"

"What the devil!" He jumped up. "What do *you* want?"

"An interview. *Your* side of the motorway dispute."

He hesitated, then waved the typist away. "All right, Nancy, you can go. Bring some coffee for Miss Armstrong."

"Three sugars," said Isa, sitting down uninvited.

She was looking very smart, in an emerald linen

trouser suit with a brilliantly patterned silk square tied, gypsy-fashion, round her small head. She was also looking very pleased with herself.

"I thought I'd get a piece about you and your son, Mr. Eldin—"

"Travers isn't here. His car got stuck in the mud yesterday, as you very well know—"

"You're not saying he got stuck too?" she enquired with mischief.

"He's had to go with one of the Land-Rovers this morning to tow it out."

"But he'll be here?"

"Later."

"I'll wait, in that case."

"We are honoured," Mr. Eldin said with an irony that covered a rising annoyance.

The coffee was brought in. Isa unwrapped the sugar cubes and dropped them in.

"You didn't give an interview to the television boys," she remarked, stirring her coffee.

"It would have been incorrect. We had a member of the Ministry of Highways with us, and he is not in a position to give interviews."

"Don't be stuffy," said Isa.

Mr. Eldin went red. "I'm not accustomed to being spoken to like that, young lady!"

"Too bad. If you hadn't got this superior attitude, you could have enlisted help from me and other journalists, ages ago."

"I don't feel in need of help, thank you."

"You don't?" She shrugged. "You amaze me. I'd say you were doing a shockingly bad public relations job."

Corinne watched her as she sipped her coffee. "You've come here to offer help to Mr. Eldin?"

"Why not?"

"Yesterday you were helping Duncan."

"That was yesterday. Round One is over. What I'm interested in now is Round Two."

"You mean you just want to see a good row?"

"That's what sells newspapers," said Isa. "A good row, or a good human interest story—something different, something *extra*. So far as I'm concerned, Duncan and his rustic cavalry have had their glory. Now if you, Mr. Eldin, can give me something as good—"

"My dear young woman, I am not going to ride about waving a banner!"

"Keep your hair on," Isa replied with a complete lack of respect. "You're awfully unimaginative! No one expects you to produce a piece of propaganda like Duncan's, and in fact it would be quite inappropriate.

"What I want from you is a good item about some farmer whose income is going to be doubled because of the motorway, or the benefits it will bring to a local hospital, or something."

"I don't go in for that kind of publicity, thank you."

"What about Travers? Can he give me any new angle?"

"My son will take his cue from me, Miss Armstrong. We have nothing to say to the press. Corinne, I see our guest has finished her refreshments, so perhaps you'll show her out!"

"Yes, sir," said Corinne, glad on her own account of a chance to escape. "This way, Isa."

With an impatient grimace Isa banged down her coffee cup and followed her to the outer office.

"Pompous old fool," she muttered.

"No, no, he can be very nice," Corinne objected.

"Only when he's getting his own way, I bet." Isa studied her. "You look a bit devastated. What's up?"

"Need you ask! Yesterday I got trapped in a protest that had nothing to do with me and appeared on TV gasping like a stranded fish, and this morning Mr. Eldin adds the *coup de grâce* by telling me who Lord Caithdale is."

"Telling you what?" Isa returned, looking momentarily puzzled. "You didn't know?"

"How could I?"

"Good heavens, I'd have thought you'd look him up. If I were new in the district I'd look up everybody in the reference books, to make sure I knew who's who and what's what."

"But you're a journalist. It never occurred to me. Honestly, Isa, I was staggered."

The other girl perched on the corner of Corinne's desk. "I don't see why," she remarked. "He may have a title, but that's *all* he's got. No money—his father threw it all away. No land—he had to sell it to pay the debts and provide an income for his mother. No home—except that barn at the back of the Burney House which he kept when he sold the rest."

"The Burney House belonged to him?"

"It was the ancestral home. The whole neighbourhood was part of the estate. Catherine's Tower—have you seen it, at the back, on the hill?—that was a Caithdale watch-tower. Which is, I suppose, why he feels so strongly about the motorway. Catherine's Tower will be knocked down, and his precious rose thicket will be ploughed up."

"And that's not all," Corinne murmured sadly.

"No? You mean the damage to the river?"

"No, there's a rare plant on the hillside—" Corinne stopped abruptly.

"Rare? How rare? Is there a story in it?"

"I've no idea, Isa. I know nothing about it, really."

"Who told you about it? Was it Duncan?" Isa looked rather angry. "Why didn't he tell *me*?"

"It's hardly newsworthy, is it?"

"It may be. Look at it this way, Corinne. There's quite a good story in the controversy over the motorway, but once the opening shots have been fired the public is going to lose interest."

"But everybody hereabouts is interested—"

"I'm not talking about *local* interest. Of course the locals are all up in arms. But that isn't enough. To make a really good impact the thing has to hit the national dailies, it has to be debated in Parliament and reach the headlines!"

"What you mean," Corinne observed with more shrewdness than usual, "is that it would do your career a lot of good if the story hit the headlines."

Isa had the grace to blush a little. "Well, that's true. But if it would be good for my career it would be even better for the Burneybank Protest Group if they could get the attention of the whole country."

"I suppose it would . . ."

"Can't you just imagine it? 'Rare Plant Threatened!' No, that's too vague. What kind of plant is it? A rose?"

"No, an orchid."

"An orchid? You're joking!"

"No, it's true. I've seen it."

The other girl narrowed her eyes. "Duncan showed it to you?"

"Yes."

There was an awkward silence. Then Isa got up and moved to the door. "It'll do a lot more good if he shows it to me. I'll go and hunt him up."

"No, Isa—he doesn't want it publicized—"

"Do you think I care what he wants? There's a story in it," said Isa, and slammed the door behind her.

When she had gone Corinne sat down at her desk, vowing that she was never going to open her mouth again to anyone about anything. Every word she spoke seemed to be giving ammunition to one person or the other. Duncan got information from her, and so did Isa. Mr. Eldin wanted to use her as a sort of ambassador. Travers misunderstood her actions even if he seemed to accept her explanations. Even dear old Mrs. Moffat had not been above taking advantage of her yesterday.

She still held in her hand her letter of resignation. She laid it on the desk in front of her. That would be the simplest solution, after all—to say "I quit!" and go back to London.

Yet strange to say, that held little attraction for her now. The three months that had gone by had brought her new interests which she would miss if she went back to London.

Moreover, there was Travers. She couldn't leave him. He needed her.

Almost at once the day became hectic. The phones began to ring and kept ringing—newspapers following up yesterday's story, officials from government departments, the local M.P., the staff of Eldin Consultants' London office, business friends, business rivals ... When Trav came in he took a hand in dealing with inquiries. There was no time for conversation until he asked her to go for a very late lunch. They went to a hotel on the edge of the town where they knew they could find a quiet corner.

"Did Dad ask you about giving us a helping hand?" he enquired.

"He began talking about it first thing, Trav. After he told me who Duncan really is. He said he thought I could speak to him—"

"And will you?"

"No!" she exclaimed. "I don't know how you can ask it!"

He pursed his lips and stared out of the window, where another rainstorm was making rivulets on the panes.

"I think you owe me that much, Corinne," he said.

Despite her cashmere sweater, she felt cold. She caught a glimpse of her reflection in the window-glass, a pale face above a blur of hyacinth blue.

"You can't deny that a lot of our problems are a result of your friendship with Donaldson," he went on. "You've chattered to him much too freely, now haven't you?"

"I admit that, Trav, but don't you see—it's for that very reason I want to steer clear of him! He's made a complete fool of me, one way or the other!"

"And I bet his conscience is giving him a lot of trouble as a result. That would make him more likely to listen to you."

"But what am I supposed to *say* to him, Trav?"

"That he's done enough harm. That he's being unfair."

"That's a matter of opinion, surely? I imagine he feels he and his friends have a perfect right to protect their environment."

"You've got to persuade him to take a wider view. It's for the good of the rest of the country."

"Maybe he'd reply that what harms one district can't be good for the rest of the country."

Trav frowned. "Listen, Corinne, it's not up to you to think up answers for him. I want you to put our case to him, and get him to call off this protest."

"He won't," she replied with certainty.

"You can at least try."

"I'd rather not. I'd feel . . . awkward."

"You didn't feel awkward about having a long talk with him on Saturday that set the whole village gossiping."

"Trav, I explained—"

"Nor on Saturday night after we said goodnight."

She made no reply, and after a moment he resumed. "According to what you told me it was all completely innocent. So why should you feel 'awkward' about approaching him on our behalf?"

She had an obscure sense that this was blackmail. Something about his whole attitude gave her a feeling of distaste. Earlier today she had been telling herself that he needed her. Was this his need? A cat's-paw to use against Duncan?

She decided to make one more try. "Don't you think it would be better to recommend another route for the motorway, Trav? You know Mrs. Moffat says the ground isn't safe, anyway."

"Mrs. Moffat? Who's she?"

"Remember, I told you about her. The old lady with gypsy ancestors—"

"Oh, for the love of Mike! You mean she's seen something in her crystal ball? Don't talk nonsense,

Corinne—the survey has shown the best and most economical route—"

"But she says the ground is hollow!"

"Then she's mistaken. The bore samples show sandstone and granite."

"But there are caves—"

"Please don't talk about things you don't understand, Corinne. Our surveys have shown us the best line for the road, and there's an end of it. Maybe it's bad luck that it's going to disturb the village of Burney, but that's progress! You've got to make Donaldson accept that."

"It will be a waste of time."

"But you'll try?"

"All right," she said unwillingly.

"Make it soon. I'd like to have something to report back to Sir James—he was furious at the way things turned out yesterday." Trav looked gloomy. "And so was Dad, until he thought it over and realized you might be able to cool things off a little with Donaldson."

"I'll speak to him this evening."

"Good girl!"

Why had she agreed? She knew it would be useless. Perhaps she had given in simply to end the wrangle—"anything for a quiet life". She felt shamed by her own weakness. But on the other hand it was going to take some hardihood to call on Duncan. Last time she saw him—in the early hours of Sunday morning—he had stalked away from her with angry disdain. She had had glimpses of him yesterday, but he had totally ignored her.

On the way home she rehearsed opening gambits to the conversation. "Good evening, Duncan, Travers sent me to talk to you about your protest campaign." "Good evening, Duncan, you're only wasting time and energy against the Ministry of Highways."

"Good evening, your Grace..." Was that how you addressed an Earl? No, no, that was a Duke. "Good evening, your Lordship... my lord..." My lord... it was unbelievable. Duncan, wandering about the hills in a Fair Isle sweater with darns in the elbow. Duncan, with a reference book on botany under his arm. Duncan, demonstrating a nice cheap car to her.

And Duncan, fixing up for Willie Stewart to attend to the faulty terminals. Duncan, arranging with Mrs. Moffat to offer her the little shepherd's cottage as a home. For he had done that. She realized it now.

Many an unseen kindness must be the result of a word dropped here, a hint spoken there. He had influence; he had helped to make life easier for her in this new setting.

Was it true, then? Did he like her?

She stopped the car and sat staring out at the rolling countryside. It was intensely green, sparkling with diamanté as the fugitive sun came and went among the rain-heavy clouds. On a far slope a little speck of black—a Border collie—darted and crept behind an erring group of sheep while on the ridge the shepherd whistled his directions. Lapwings were calling in the distance.

A beautiful land. His land. No wonder he was so fiercely protective towards it. If in defence of it he used any weapon that came to hand—if he used Corinne herself—who could blame him?

And that thought recalled her to herself. Certainly he "liked" her. He had said it, in a way: "You really are an extraordinarily pretty girl." That was his estimate of her. She was pretty and young and a new face in the district. Quite worth kissing if the occasion arose.

But it was absurd to build any hopes on that; it would be like building a house on sand. Perhaps they might have built up a real friendship if things had been different, but in the circumstances that could never happen now. They were on opposite sides of the fence, in the middle of a bitter controversy. This wasn't a time to hope for friendship, a time

> When hard words, jealousies, and fears
> Set folks together by the ears.

In an effort to bolster up her defences, for which she mocked herself while she did it, she went home and changed from the workaday sweater and matching skirt to a delicate black-and-white voile dress. The evening was really too cool for it, but she knew it made her tawny hair look richer and her grey eyes darker. Her excuse to herself was that after she had spoken to Duncan she was going to treat herself to dinner in the hotel restaurant.

Once again she began to rehearse conversational openings as she rang the old iron bell-pull outside his door. But they all flew out of her head as she heard his feet clatter on the stairs and next moment he was staring at her, first in surprise and then in anger.

"So it's you!" he exclaimed. "And what do you want?"

"I w—wondered if I could have a w—word with you ..."

"And I want a word with you. Come on." He took her by the arm, not very gently, and urged her up the stairs.

She understood why when she came into the big

living-room. Isa Armstrong was there, looking cross and flustered.

"What are you doing here?" she demanded in annoyance.

"I . . . I . . ."

"I'll ask the questions, if you don't mind, Isa." Duncan turned a stony gaze on Corinne. "Isa says you told her about the orchid."

The memory of that involuntary disclosure had come back to Corinne's mind once or twice during the day: she had known instinctively that that was the reason for Isa's presence now.

"It slipped out," she confessed. "But I didn't say any more than that. And, in fact, Duncan—it ought to be a help, not a hindrance."

"A help to what, in heaven's name?"

"Well, as Isa was saying to me, it might catch the national interest. If, as you told me, it only grows in three other places in the British Isles—"

"Be quiet!" he cut in.

"Aha!" Isa crowed. "Only three other places, eh? Where, for instance?"

"I haven't the slightest intention of telling you! It would help you to identify it."

"I can't understand why you're being so stubborn about it, Duncan."

"That's because, although you may know a lot about reporting, you know nothing about ecology. You already know the plant is rare. It's also vulnerable—"

"To changes that would come about if they took road-building equipment up on the hillside, yes," Corinne intervened. "But what harm can it do just to *tell* Isa about it?"

" 'Just tell her'—you must be extremely naïve,"

Duncan said to her. "Isa wants to take a photographer on to the growing site and take pictures. Can you imagine what would happen next? Gangs of casual picnickers, tramping all over the hill looking for it. Worse still, *finding* it!"

"Why shouldn't they?" demanded Isa. "They've as much right to look at it as you have, surely? Don't be such a dog in the manger!"

He frowned angrily. "Have you ever seen the damage done in a bluebell wood by casual pickers? There are coppices and spinneys in southern England where bluebells have died out because unthinking idiots pulled the plants up by the roots."

"But no one would pull up an orchid," said Corinne.

"Do you want to bet?"

"Oh, come on, Duncan. Even if they did, it would grow again."

"It wouldn't, Isa. It *wouldn't*."

Corinne could see her hesitate. "Well then," she said, "that's a risk we have to take."

"Why do we have to?"

"Because publishing this story would be a master stroke in your campaign—and without full details and a picture, it's only half a story."

"No, Isa."

She moved angrily. "Don't be a fool, Duncan. Hang it all, it's only a flower, after all."

Corinne knew, from the look on his face, that he was struggling not to say some very bitter things. At last he said, "You have no real conscience, Isa. No real concern—"

"That's not true! I've played my part in the protest—"

"Only because it made a good news item. If you

could get something as good or better from the other side, you'd be just as enthusiastic about putting their case."

Isa shot a warning glance at Corinne which said plainly: "Don't tell him what I said to Mr. Eldin!" To Duncan she retorted: "Well, that's my job!"

"Exactly. And that's why I'm not going to tell you about the orchid—I regard it as *my* job to safeguard it."

"I think you're attaching too much importance to it."

"That's what people have been saying for generations, and look what they've done to our countryside! Plants and trees that used to be common have vanished. Hedgerows that gave shelter to birds and insects are rooted up to make bigger fields, and what happens?—the wind blows and blows with nothing to stop it and the soil is whirled away. Men with guns used to go out shooting. Collectors paid boys to climb trees and rob nests. As a result we've lost dozens of birds that belonged here. Where are the falcons, where are the eagles? We have to build a *fortress* round the osprey . . ."

Isa had the grace to look abashed. "See here, Duncan, I'm not indifferent to the environment," she muttered. "I'm willing to talk to my editor about your precious orchid and get him to run the story as a big environmental issue. It's very trendy these days to be on the side of the environmentalists—"

He cut her short by striding to the door and flinging it wide. "Please go, Isa. The more you say the less I want to hear." And as Corinne moved uncertainly he added, "You too. If you came to apologize for giving Isa the information, you're much too late."

In silence the two girls descended the stairs together. "Phew," said Isa as they hesitated before going out into the rainy evening, "he can be very icy when the frost sets in!"

Corinne shivered in her filmy dress—but whether from Duncan's dismissal or from the weather, she didn't know.

"Cold?" Isa asked. "Come on, let's have a cup of coffee or something."

They made a dash through the steely rain to the hotel, arriving breathless and damp. Nell, seeing them as they came in, hustled them into the lounge.

"Come away in by the fire! Terrible weather for August, is it no? I hear the burns are all overflowing already, and the Caith Water is up by the banks. There now . . . comfy?"

"Oh, that's lovely," said Corinne, stretching out her hands to the cheerful log fire in the great iron fire-basket. "What a blessing it is to get cosy. Does it often rain like this?"

"Och, in hill country the clouds are always likely to drop down a shower or two. You'll see—it'll be fair and fine the morn. Now then, what can I get you?"

They decided on coffee and sandwiches. Isa took off her silk square and spread it on the back of a chair to dry. She stared into the fire. "He's really angry with me this time," she said moodily.

" 'This time'? You sound as if you had frequent . . . er . . . disagreements?"

"You can say that again!" She sighed. "I suppose we know each other too well . . . We've been friends since childhood, you know."

"No, I didn't know."

"Oh yes. I had a terrible crush on him in my teens." She laughed without much amusement. "To tell you the truth, I was pretty sure of myself as the future Lady Caithdale. But it didn't happen."

Corinne was longing to ask why not, but it seemed a cruel question. After a moment Isa continued unasked: "I think he was fond of me. Certainly there wasn't anybody else in the running. But then his father died and there was endless trouble over death duties and debts and goodness knows what else. When he surfaced again out of all that... well, I seemed to have lost my place."

"That must have hurt you," Corinne murmured.

"Hurt me?" The other girl considered that. "I don't know. I think it made me stubborn—what they call 'fechty' hereabouts. I was determined to hang on to him by whatever contact there was left."

She shook her head. Corinne made a sympathetic sound.

"The truth of it is, we're too like one another," Isa said. "He can see through me because he understands how my mind works. We both have a streak of determination, of... of..."

"Ruthlessness?" Corinne suggested.

Isa gave her a sharp glance. "Do you think I'm ruthless?"

"I think you want very much to succeed."

"Ah. There's where Duncan and I differ. He doesn't give a hang about success." She frowned and rubbed her chilly hands. "Do you know, he could have made quite a comfortable income if he'd used his title and gone on the boards of various companies. But he wouldn't. He won't even use 'Caithdale' for selling his stupid old tractors. He says people round here know who he is—and if they don't it doesn't matter."

"I think that's rather admirable."

Nell arrived with a big pot of coffee and spent some time fussing over them as she set out cups on a nearby table before drawing it near them. "I'll bring the sandwiches in a meenit. You can be comfy here for a whilie yet—most of the people in the restaurant havena reached their second course yet."

"Thank you, Nell."

"It's a pleasure, Miss Lenwood."

When she had left them Isa said abruptly: "You like Duncan a lot."

"Me?"

"Yes, you! Your face a minute ago, when he showed you the door!"

"Well," Corinne said, blushing, "it wasn't very pleasant."

Isa smiled. "You take things too much to heart.. Fancy getting in a state about some silly old flower!"

"But it's important, Isa."

"Not to me!"

"Well, it is to me."

"Really? I didn't know you were interested in botany?"

Corinne busied herself with the coffee pot, avoiding a reply. What could she say? She wasn't interested in botany; she could only remember a few of the basics from school lessons—the coloured diagrams of the wall charts, the lists of names of plants . . .

But she liked flowers, always had. And this particular flower was rare, and Duncan wanted to protect it.

It came to her in a sudden flash of understanding that made her hand shake as she poured the coffee: the orchid was important to her because it was important to Duncan!

Isa accepted her cup, dropping three sugar lumps into

it. She watched the turbulence made by her spoon as she stirred. She was clearly deep in thought.

"It must be a very pretty flower, I suppose?" she said at length.

"We-ell ... It *is* pretty, but not astonishingly so."

"I wish I could see it. Will you take me there, Corinne?"

Corinne was startled. "Certainly not!" she exclaimed.

"Why not?"

"Because Duncan doesn't want its whereabouts known."

"Why should you care?" Isa asked.

Once again she didn't know how to answer.

"Listen," Isa said. "I'll make a bargain with you. You show me where the orchid is growing, and in exchange I'll tell you something I think you'd very much like to know."

"About what?"

"About Duncan."

Corinne avoided looking at the other girl. Instead she concentrated on watching the tide of red that came and went among the logs in the fire-basket. "I can't imagine why you should imagine there's anything about Duncan that particularly interests me."

"No?" Isa gave a little laugh. "I'll tell you the answer to that free of charge."

Corinne shook her head vehemently. "I don't really want to discuss it."

"Afraid?"

"Really, Isa, I don't know what you mean."

"Perhaps you don't ... I believe you actually don't know," Isa murmured, a little taken aback.

"Don't know *what*? What are you talking about?"

"My dear girl," Isa said, "you're in love with him."

CHAPTER NINE

LUCKILY at that moment Nell arrived with the sandwiches. A complete silence fell as she set them down. She glanced curiously from one girl to the other but, unusual for her, said nothing.

"It's true, isn't it?" Isa insisted. "You've gone quite overboard for him."

"No! No, no—you don't know how wrong you are! As a matter of fact—" she caught herself up just as she was about to say it was impossible for her to have any feelings about Duncan because she was engaged to Travers. But the engagement had to remain a secret.

"All I can say is that you're talking complete rubbish," she said angrily.

"'The lady protests too much, methinks'," Isa quoted. "I suppose it *is* a shock if you hadn't suspected it before."

"There's nothing to suspect! I don't know whatever gave you such a comical idea!"

"I'll tell you, if you like. Every time he frowns at you, you look desolate. Your anxiety on his behalf is obvious. And whatever he says, you take as if it were handed down from Mount Zion."

"I don't want to discuss it. You're completely mistaken."

"Don't you want to know what I could tell you about *him*?"

"No," Corinne said, making a great effort at recapturing her self-control. "I think you're just mischief-making, Isa, as you so often are. Now drink your coffee and have a sandwich and stop being silly."

"Hoity-toity!" said Isa, raising her brows. But she could tell that she had lost the advantage that her shock tactics had momentarily given her. While she was still considering what to do next and Corinne was eyeing her warily, there came a welcome interruption.

Trav came into the lounge and, seeing them, came straight over to them. Isa beckoned him to the sofa beside her. "I came to see you today at the office, but you weren't there. Got your car back?"

He nodded. "Conditions were a bit better this morning—most of the water had drained away, so we didn't have too much trouble pulling it out."

"Is Sir James Prudholme coming back to go over the route some other day?"

"No comment!"

"Is the Ministry going to issue a statement?"

"You'd better ask the Ministry."

"I did. They said 'No comment'!"

Trav laughed. "But that doesn't put you off in the slightest, does it?"

"Why should it? There's a story in this thing, still waiting to be told. I'll get it no matter what anyone says."

"Round Two," murmured Corinne.

"What?" said Travers with a glance at her.

"This morning Isa said Round One was yesterday, and what she's interested in now is Round Two. But your father made the same reply—no comment."

"You talked to my father?" Trav said.

"Don't sound so apprehensive. Your father's only a man like the rest. If we prick him, does he not bleed? as Shakespeare very nearly said."

"I wonder he didn't shrivel you up into cinders. I can tell you I was quite glad of the excuse to keep out of his way this morning."

Isa gave him a sarcastic smile. "You know your

trouble?" she remarked. "You take your father at his own estimation."

"Well, he *is* quite a personage. He had a successful career in the Army and then, quite late in life, built up a very lucrative business from scratch."

"Bully for him! But that doesn't make him Superman, you know." Isa patted him on the hand then got to her feet. "Well, I've come to the end of a perfect day. Not a single useful piece of copy... So long, everybody."

Trav watched her make her way to the door. "She's quite a girl. I wish she were on our side in this fight."

"I think she'd come over to your side quite quickly if you offered her the right inducement."

"What do you mean?"

"A story. Something she could print. She's a reporter first and foremost."

"Oh, I don't know," said Trav. "She seems a very glamorous sort of girl to me."

All at once an extraordinary thought came into Corinne's mind: that Isa would be the right sort of person for Trav. Someone to give him backbone, to make him see his alarming parent in a proper perspective.

She gave a little gasp at the idea. What was so extraordinary was that the thought caused her no pain at all. She was able to picture Isa Armstrong at Trav's side without the slightest twinge of jealousy or surge of anxiety.

She didn't love him! That was the long and the short of it. The first seeds of doubt, planted in her mind by Duncan a couple of nights ago, had grown now to a complete realization.

What was it Isa had said about herself and Duncan? "We're too like one another . . ."

That was the trouble with the relationship between Travers and Corinne: they were too like one another. Corinne was unable to help him in the way he needed. He was too diffident, too unsure of himself in the face of opposition. His father's attitude made things worse for him, but instead of helping him to fight back Corinne was a handicap to him.

She knew that Norman Eldin was never going to be "in the right mood" to be told of their engagement. He didn't want his son to marry his secretary. Isa, in Corinne's place, would have barged into his office and said, "Mr. Eldin, Trav and I are getting married in six weeks," and no matter what the battles and storms, the marriage would have taken place. That was the essential difference between them: Isa didn't care about upsetting or annoying other people, whereas Corinne was made miserable by discord.

It was unlucky for Trav that he chose to fall in love with her. She was quite the wrong sort of girl for him.

And, equally important, he was quite the wrong sort of man for her. All his doubts and uncertainties would reflect on to her own personality, magnifying a natural diffidence that might quite easily turn into timidity. She realized that in the year since she had been working with him she had assumed the tactics of always avoiding trouble if she could; she had turned into something of a chameleon, taking on protective colouring when necessary. In previous jobs she had been less quiescent: in fact she had walked out of one at a moment's notice, on a matter of principle. How greatly she had allowed him to influence her already!

Now that the realization had come to her she knew

she must tell Trav. She couldn't bear to let things go on a moment longer.

"Come out for a walk, Trav," she suggested.

"What? On a grey evening like this?"

"But I want to talk to you. It's important."

"Go ahead, then."

"Not here, Trav. Let's go somewhere else."

He drew his brows together in perplexity. "I can't do that. I'm waiting for Dad."

"Oh, *Trav*!"

"What's the matter?"

"Can't you do anything without reference to your father?" she burst out.

He looked both hurt and surprised. "It happens to be important. He's telephoning Sir James Prudholme at his hotel at this very moment."

"Whatever he's doing, you don't have to hang around here waiting for him."

"He's expecting to find me here," he said stubbornly.

Corinne drew a deep breath. "Trav, I want to have an important talk with you. Please come."

"You're just being awkward. Why can't you say what you have to say here and now?"

"All right." She paused. "You know that ring we were going to buy?"

He looked blank for a moment, then recovered. "Oh, that's what's bothering you! Look, I know we said we'd go to Edinburgh—"

"That's what I'm trying to tell you, Trav. There's no need. I've changed my mind."

She was afraid that was too cruel, but in fact it didn't really come home to him. "Changed your mind about what?" he queried.

"About . . . about getting married. About even getting engaged."

"Corinne!" *Now* he understood, and his smooth features went momentarily haggard. "You're not serious?"

"I'm afraid I am. I realize now that it's all been a terrible mistake."

"But how can you say that? You love me and I love you."

"No." She shook her head. "I thought I loved you, Trav, and I'm very sorry for appearing heartless now, but . . . but somehow everything is different now. Perhaps I know myself better. Since I came to Burney—"

"Yes, that's what it is!" he broke in angrily. "Everything's changed since we came here!"

Other people were drifting into the lounge. They cast interested glances towards them.

"We can't talk here, Trav," she urged. "Come out for a walk."

"I've told you already, I can't do that. And if all you want to do is go on with this nonsense, I can't see why I should!"

"It isn't nonsense. I'm in earnest."

"If you ask me you've taken leave of your senses—"

"It's no use getting angry. That won't help. If you would only understand—"

But Mr. Eldin joined them at that moment, drowning out her plea with irritated complaints about Prudholme's coldness on the telephone. "As if it was *my* fault that the local TV company was on hand . . ."

"Are you coming, Trav?" Corinne said, moving away.

"Coming?" echoed his father. "Where? You and I have work to do, my boy."

173

And since Trav did nothing to gainsay that, Corinne turned her back and went out.

She crossed the vestibule, reached the entrance steps, and then was at a momentary stop at sight of Duncan sprinting up the drive with a mackintosh held loosely over his head to keep off the rain.

Seeing her, he called, "Corinne!"

But the last thing she wanted was to be directed back indoors to the hotel lounge. Disregarding him, she made a dash for her car. She had just wrenched open its door and got in when he reached her.

"Corinne, don't go! I want to talk to you—"

"But I don't want to talk to *you*!" she returned. "I'm going home."

"Corinne—" He reached in to grasp her wrist as she switched on the ignition.

"Let go! How dare you!" She jerked up her hand so that his grasp was shaken off.

"But I wanted to say—"

"I don't care what you wanted to say!" Next moment she was off down the drive in a spray of wet gravel.

In the rear mirror she saw him stare after her, and then set off like a deer across the lawn. She realized he was going to vault the low wall that bordered the garden, at the point where she would pass it if she headed for home. So instead she swung the wheel to the left, and went through the village and off up the glen road.

The rain slacked off after a moment, but there were heavy clouds on the upper slopes of the hills. The whole landscape looked saturated. The time was about eight o'clock, with the light fading more rapidly than normal because the sky was so grey although sunset was still about an hour away.

As she drove Corinne became calmer. She had left the hotel lounge in a state of indignation at Trav's spinelessness, then almost immediately been overtaken by something like panic when Duncan called to her. Why, she didn't quite know. She had had a dreadful fear that she might blurt out something she would regret.

But what? What, actually, could there be between them that evoked so much alarm on her part?

Had she been afraid she would say: "I've broken off with Trav because it's you I love"?

Nonsense. He was nothing to her, nothing at all. His behaviour to her earlier in the evening had been unfriendly, to say the least, and she for her part had no wish for his company after being shown the door.

"My dear girl, you're in love with him." What had made Isa say that? Isa was observant and shrewd: had there really been any grounds for her accusation?

"I don't love him, I don't!" she told herself fiercely. "He's nothing to me!"

For it would be so humiliating to love a man who told here to her face that she was naïve and silly, and tricked her quite shamelessly when he wanted to get information out of her.

Yet as she drove over the ridge to the next valley, she was haunted by the sound of his voice saying: "Corinne, don't go! I want to talk to you." And, from farther away, in a gentler tone: "You really are the most extraordinarily pretty girl . . ."

She wouldn't think about him. And really it would be better if she didn't, for there were sheets of rainwater on the road which needed her attention as she reached the floor of the valley. The road surface had been damaged by the collected rain—if that was what it was?

When she came slowly into sight of the river she

realized that the pools on the road were not rain. The Caith Water had overflowed its banks at some time during the day and though the stream had gone down a little it was still pouring in an energetic torrent over the bridge she was about to cross.

She drew up to study it. Probably her little saloon could force its way across, but if the water got into the engine ... She didn't fancy being stuck in the middle of the bridge until the next driver came along to shunt her over.

There was another bridge higher up, not much of an engineering feat but standing higher above the water; she believed it had been constructed for driving the flocks down from the upper pastures. If she turned to the west along the track by the Burneybank, she would come to the Sheep Bridge.

She'd better get a move on. The cloud was rolling down the hill towards her—rain and mist, limiting her visibility to about twenty yards. Still, part of the route would be marked by the posts put in by the Eldin survey team, for it was the route of the motorway. She had her headlights on now, ready to pick up each slim red-and-white marker.

The track up the Burneybank was sticky; her wheels caught and churned in the mud. But the stalwart little car shouldered on through the cloud without the engine missing a beat.

There was the first marker. She would be on a level contour for about half a mile now. There were big puddles on the road which reflected like silver in her lamps and made a strange drumming noise as she drove through.

For one strange moment she saw ahead of her that

the water was moving, and thought, "That's odd—this is level ground, so why is it running downhill?"

Then there was a strange slithering, scrambling slide and the steering-wheel ceased to answer. She jammed on the brakes, but incredibly, there was nothing for the wheels to pull up on. Incredibly, the track had gone, the ground had gone, and the car was falling, falling. Incredibly, she was heading into a gaping hole.

Corinne screamed and reached for the door handle. But earth and stones were already closing in against the door. It wouldn't open. She shoved against it, releasing her safety belt with the other hand.

But then the car tilted over on its side and she was thrown like a doll against the passenger door. Her head hit the window.

Then there was blackness.

CHAPTER TEN

CORINNE was only unconscious for a few minutes. When she opened her eyes the first thing she saw was the car windscreen above her head. That, of course, was absurd—windscreens are ahead of you, not above you. Then, slowly, she realized that she was lying in a huddle against the door of the car—the handle was pressing into the small of her back.

She pulled herself up on her elbow. The glass of the door by the driver's seat was stove in by rocks and earth; as she stared at it the glass fragments began to part and fall inwards, letting a cascade of soil come in to spatter on her face. Luckily, for the present it went no farther: she didn't think it would be very pleasant if one of those small boulders crashed in on her.

How was she going to get out? The door opposite was jammed by the weight of soil. How about the door beneath her? Gingerly she turned her head. Through the glass beneath her she could see nothing at all—only blackness.

That was when the hideous realization hit her. Mrs. Moffat had talked about "hollowness" beneath the motorway's planned route. Corinne's car was tipped on its side over a hole many feet deep, a hole in the roof of a cave beneath the Burneybank.

The caves had been mentioned now and again as the refuge of the Borderers of long ago. Probably the streams that eventually reached the valleys had bored these channels underground in prehistoric times. Below Corinne's car there might be emptiness, or an underground stream.

She stared round the inside of the Renault. Light— failing daylight—was coming in only at the front. The back window was obscured by soil, as was the side opposite to where she was lying. Beneath her there was, so far as she could tell, nothingness. The car was wedged in the loose earth at the lip of the cave-in by its left side and the back. The only way out was through the windscreen.

That being so, she would have to break it. But with what?

Windscreen glass is shatter-proof. It would need some heavy implement, and more strength than Corinne possessed, to knock a hole in it.

But the alternative was to wait here until someone came by—and when would that be? She tried to see the time on her wrist-watch, but the crystal had been shattered in the accident. It was probably about eight-thirty. Already twilight lay over the rectangle she could see through the windscreen and in half an hour it would be dark. Almost certainly, no one would be out on the Burneybank in this weather and at this hour of night; even the shepherd she had seen earlier would be at home now, the collie sleeping on his feet as he smoked an evening pipe.

So she must try to break the windscreen unless she wanted to stay here all night. She squirmed round to feel in the glove compartment for a tool of some sort. All she found was maps, a pair of sunglasses, and the first-aid box.

Anything on the back window-ledge? If there had been, it had been thrown to the floor in the fall. She decided to feel about on the floor, but as she moved the vehicle lurched : there was a slither of gravel. She froze. With one or two little creaking sounds the car became motionless again.

For quite a long time after that she held her breath. She was terrified that movement of air through her lungs would make some disastrous difference to the car's position. Then, painfully, she relaxed.

The situation had been dramatically demonstrated to her. So long as she stayed where she was, lying against the lower window, the car would stay where it was. If she altered her position, the car would move.

How long would it stay like that? The rain was still falling, making the ground soft and malleable—if there were any more subsidence because of gathering moisture, who knew what might happen?

Time passed. It grew darker outside. Then it dawned on Corinne that though it must be night, she could still see light through the windscreen. What could that be?

The car headlights! They were still switched on, and the angle at which the car had settled was sending the beam obliquely upward, to be reflected back in a soft haze by the mist.

She felt a leap of hope. Perhaps it would be visible from the road below!

Perhaps... If anyone was driving by on a rainy misty night.

When at last the sound came it alarmed her terribly. She thought it was some sound of stress in the Renault. She tensed, waiting for the final slide downward that would take her to oblivion.

But the vehicle remained unmoving. The sound grew a little louder.

It was a motor engine.

Corinne drew in a deep breath, intending to shout for help. Then the uselessness of it occurred to her, and she remained voiceless, listening.

The sound stopped. Despair clutched her.

Then, muffled by the cocoon around her, she heard a voice.

"Corinne! Corinne!"

Now she would shout. If she could hear him, he might hear her. "Help! I'm here! Help!"

She heard a scrambling sound, the voice coming nearer—and then the Renault shuddered and began to tilt. The voice stopped abruptly.

There was a long pause. Then she heard: "Corinne, are you there? Corinne, it's me—Duncan!"

"Yes! Yes, I'm here. Trapped in the car."

"Thank God! I thought perhaps... Corinne, when I

tried to get to the car bonnet the ground began to give way."

"I know. If I move the same thing happens."

Another pause.

"Listen, I've got a rope in my car. I'm going to tow you out. But the problem is, how am I going to attach the rope?"

"Duncan, be careful! Don't come near! Oh, darling, stay clear!"

There was no answer. She heard disconnected sounds, indistinct and varying, as if he were moving about some yards away. The car engine started up.

"Corinne, are you listening?"

"Yes!"

"I think we're only going to get one chance at this. I've got the rope running round the base of thorn bushes farther up the hill. I'm going to use that to take my weight so as not to put pressure on the ground by the edge of the gap. Do you understand?"

"Yes."

"I'm going to drop a loop of rope round your front bumper and then pull myself clear. Darling, the car may drop a bit. Try not to be afraid."

"I won't be, Duncan."

"It won't take long. Then I'm going to drive my car back from the gap. Okay?"

"Okay."

She tried to picture what was happening. He had the rope attached to something at the front of his own vehicle, then going up the hillside to the "hitch": from there the rope came down again to the track, and was to be fastened to the front of the Renault—if he could do it.

Suddenly she was filled with terror for him. If her car were to go, she at least was protected inside it to some extent. But if the land subsided when he was at the edge, he would go down in a smothering rush of rocks to the darkness below.

"Duncan, don't try it!" she called. But there was no reply.

A moment later there was a long tremor through the soil. For an instant she saw Duncan's head silhouetted against the soft haze outside the windscreen. There was a thud as his hand glanced off the metal of the front grille.

A rush of movement followed. The Renault seemed to swoop downward about a foot. Corinne's heart came into her mouth. She thought: "This is the end."

Then the movement stopped with a jerk. Soil slipped all around her, the far window came in with a rush, but the car stayed in place. Then there was a roar of noise, Duncan's car dragging backwards at full power.

The Renault edged sideways and upwards. It began to roll over on to solid ground. Corinne clutched at the back of the seat nearest the door where she had been lying. The car came to a standstill.

She heard running footsteps. The door was wrenched open. Duncan's arms were around her.

"Quick!" he said. "Out—before the rest of the ground gives way!"

His arm urging her along the hillside, she stumbled at his side. They slithered down the slope to his car. He had left it, engine running, doors open. He cut the rope free from the front, threw himself in beside her, and reversed at speed down the track.

With a smothered roar, the lights of the Renault semaphored in the sky, then vanished. The little saloon went down in a landslip that took ten square yards of the surface with it.

Corinne hid her face against Duncan's chest. "It's all right," he murmured, "you're safe, it's all right."

"Oh, Duncan, you might have been *killed*!"

"Now, now, that's all over. Good heavens, you're shivering . . ." He pulled off his jacket to wrap it round her, then held her close. "Don't ever frighten me like that again!" he said.

As if in a dream Corinne watched the road slip by under the wheels. The houses of the village appeared, the friendly windows gleaming with lamplight; then the Burney House. Duncan helped her out. She caught a glimpse of Mrs. Patterson's anxious face as she hurried to greet them.

When Corinne opened her eyes she was in the room she had first occupied in the hotel. The sun was shining, making a pattern on the carpet. A shadow moved on it. She raised herself on her elbow : Mrs. Patterson had just opened the curtains.

"So there you are!" Mrs. Patterson said gently. "How do you feel?"

"Stiff."

"No wonder. Dr. Blake said you'd had a terrible shaking."

Corinne lay back. Images of last night formed themselves behind her closed lids.

"Are you ready for breakfast?"

She suddenly realized she was starving. "I'll be down in a minute," she declared, preparing to get up.

"No, no, stay where you are! The doctor said you were to have breakfast in bed and in any case, it's after eleven—the restaurant's closed. And you've no clothes yet. Mrs. Moffat is going to bring a case from your cottage."

Corinne glanced down at herself. She was wearing a pretty sprigged cotton nightdress. "Whose is this?"

"Mine, and very welcome you are."

"Thank you, Mrs. Patterson." She felt foolish tears come into her eyes. She swallowed hard, then asked tremulously, "Is Duncan all right?"

"Apart from being in a great taking over your mishap and some bad scratches on his hands," Mrs. Patterson said with a quizzical smile, "he's fine. He asked me to let him know when you'd had breakfast, so he could come to see you."

"Would...would you tell him I'm anxious to see him?"

"I think he knows that," said Mrs. Patterson.

When the door opened again it was Isa Armstrong, carrying the breakfast tray. "Good morning! That was quite a drama, wasn't it?"

"It was dreadful," Corinne agreed with a shudder.

"Fresh toast—I made it with my own fair hands."

Corinne pushed back her hair and stared at her. "Why?"

"Because Mrs. Patterson's busy with lunch preparations."

"No, why are you— Oh, I see. I'm a news story, am I?"

"And how!" Isa agreed. "What do you think?—it looks as if the route for the motorway is a complete washout! They should have asked old Meg Moffat— she says there are caves and hollows all along the Burneybank."

"Oh, goodness, Mr. Eldin must be furious!"

"So I gather. Poor old Trav! I've offered to hold his hand if he needs comfort."

"Have you indeed?" Corinne murmured, amused.

"It doesn't perturb you?"

"Not a bit."

"Mmm," said Isa. "I've an idea, from things I heard about your arrival with Duncan last night, that you've found out for yourself what I offered to tell you, about Duncan's feelings for you."

Corinne busied herself buttering her toast.

"Don't want to talk about it? Well," Isa shrugged, "perhaps you're right. Let's talk about the accident. Give me all the dramatic details to build up into a front-page splash . . ."

Corinne obliged. Isa took notes and ate two pieces of her toast. She was making her go over it a second time "for highlights", as she termed it, when a tap on the door heralded Mrs. Moffat with Corinne's overnight bag.

"Here I am wi' your clothes, my lass," she said, bustling in. "How's yourself?"

"I'm fine, thanks. Got a few bruises, but nothing to complain of. It's kind of you to bring my things, Mrs. Moffat. Who suggested it?"

"Who do you think?" the old lady said, setting the bag down with a thump.

"Himself?" asked Corinne, smiling.

"None other. And tell me this, Isabel Armstrong," she said, wheeling on Isa, "what are you doing here bothering this poor lass with your wee notebook?"

"I'm getting an exclusive story, Meg."

"Well, you've got as much as you're going to. Off with you, and let the girl have some peace."

"Do you want me to fetch Duncan to you?"

Isa raised her hands in a gesture of surrender. "All right, all right, 'The Armstrongs are flying', as the ballad says. The last thing I want is the rough side of Duncan's tongue."

She closed her notebook as if to go, but filched another piece of toast as she went.

"Away wi' you!" cried Mrs. Moffat, making shooing gestures at her.

"'Bye!" said Isa. "I'll send a photographer later for a picture of the happy pair."

"Oh, now look here, Meg—"

Mrs. Moffat was laughing as the door closed on her, but became serious as she looked at Corinne.

"I'm happy for you," she said. "And for him."

"Oh, Mrs. Moffat... Aren't you all taking an awful lot for granted?"

"Some things are like that. I take it for granted that it'll be dark at night and light in the daytime."

"But Meg... nothing's been *said* ..."

"Oh, havers," Meg replied. "Get yourself up and dressed. If you've finished with that tray, I'll tak' it— nothing makes a room look worse than dirty plates." She picked it up and was on her way, but paused at the door. "I hope I've brought the right clothes. This is a day you want to look your prettiest."

With a strangely beating heart Corinne set about making ready for the day. She felt strange—a little light-headed. She told herself it was the after-effects of the accident, but she knew that wasn't true.

When she had showered she put on the dress that Mrs. Moffat had chosen: with an unerring instinct the old lady had brought a simple shirtwaister of dark blue cotton and a floral ribbon to tie back her hair.

After she had dressed Corinne hesitated. Should she go downstairs?

No, she would wait. She sat down, her hands in her lap.

About five minutes later there was a knock on the door. "Come in," she called. Even his knock on a door was unmistakable.

"Good morning, Duncan," she said.

He crossed to stand looking down at her in her chair by the window. "You look flushed," he said. "Are you feverish?"

"No, I'm quite well."

"There are reporters downstairs, wanting to speak to you."

She smiled. A strange feeling of confidence had come to her. "Let them wait," she said. "I think perhaps you want to speak to me first."

"I wanted to speak to you last night—to apologize to you for being rude earlier. But you wouldn't listen."

"It was a bad moment," she told him. "I'd just explained to Trav that he needn't buy me an engagement ring."

"The engagement is ended?" It was a statement rather than a question.

"I don't think it was ever begun, Duncan. But even so, I hadn't enjoyed the scene with Trav... And Isa had been saying things that upset me."

"I could see you were upset. That was why I decided to come after you."

"Lucky that you did. I wouldn't be here now, otherwise."

He held out his hands to her. "Lucky for me, my darling. The luckiest thing I ever did."

Swept up and into his arms, she abandoned herself

to his kisses. She wanted him to know beyond the need of words that she belonged to him, now and for ever. The tension that had existed between them was changed now, into a bond of precious metal that would never let them go.

"My darling, my love," she murmured as she cradled his hands against her cheeks, those hands scarred and cut from last night's dangers. "I only understood my real feelings when I thought you might be killed!"

"Hush, don't think about that." He drew her near, to drop kisses on her cheekbones. "I always knew you were the only one for me."

"Really, Duncan?"

"From the very first, when you appeared out of the mist by the rose thicket. To me you were the perfect girl—my rose among the roses."

"I remember . . . You used those very words to me."

"I've thought of you like that ever since—my gentle girl, my sweet and gentle girl, like a burnet blossom. I wanted to protect you . . ."

"And you did. You were so kind to me, Duncan—"

"Nonsense! I was a brute! But I suppose . . . I was just plain jealous."

"Were you?" She looked up, a spark of mischief in her eyes. "That never occurred to me!"

"When I saw that idiot making you miserable . . . ! I was sometimes tempted to wring his neck."

"But he didn't do anything, really—"

"Oh yes, he did. Don't defend him. You were often very depressed because of things he said or did. But he doesn't matter any more," said Duncan. "He and all his foolish plans are a thing of the past for us. The roses will grow on the Burneybank and the sun will shine on them—and we'll go together to look at them, you and I."

"The rainbow comes and goes,

And lovely is the rose," Corinne quoted. "It's wonderful to think our roses won't be ploughed up. I should have hated that. And the special orchid, the ladies' tresses—they'll be unharmed. They'll bloom again next year, won't they? The landslip won't discourage them?"

"Who knows?" he said. "Next year we'll go and look." He paused a moment. "You do want to live at Burney? Perhaps I shouldn't forget to ask your preference about our future home."

There was no need to answer that in words. At length, reluctantly, he let her go.

"We ought to go downstairs and face the music, I suppose. Do you feel up to it, Corinne?"

"I suppose so," she sighed. "But you'll do all the talking, won't you, darling?"

"I'll say as little as possible. The sooner we can get out of the public eye, the sooner we can get married."

"Oh," gasped Corinne. A frightening thought had struck her. She would be Lady Caithdale!

"What's the matter?" He paused as he was about to lead her out of the room. As if by telepathy he guessed what she was thinking. "Don't let it frighten you," he said teasingly. "Hereabouts they'll just refer to you as Herself!"

Later, as she sat apparently unnoticed while the reporters talked to Duncan, old Mrs. Moffat came quietly to her side. She took Corinne's hand and kissed her gently on the cheek.

"There now," she murmured in triumph, "did I not tell you that come the winter you wouldna be in my shepherd's cottage?"

Corinne smiled. "You foresaw it all, Mrs. Moffat, didn't you?"

"For sure. I have the gift."

"What do you foresee in the future for us?"

"Och," the old lady said, "it needs no second sight to tell you that. You'll be blessed, my dear. Love is its own blessing."

And looking across the room to catch the eye of this man so inexpressibly dear to her, Corinne knew the old gypsy woman was right.

16 GREAT RE-ISSUES

Here is a wonderful opportunity to read many of the Harlequin Romances you may have missed.

- ☐ 917 TIMBER MAN
      Joyce Dingwell
- ☐ 920 MAN AT MULERA
      Kathryn Blair
- ☐ 926 MOUNTAIN MAGIC
      Susan Barrie
- ☐ 944 WHISPER OF DOUBT
      Andrea Blake
- ☐ 973 TIME OF GRACE
      Sara Seale
- ☐ 976 FLAMINGOS ON THE LAKE
      Isobel Chace
- ☐ 980 A SONG BEGINS
      Mary Burchell
- ☐ 992 SNARE THE WILD HEART
      Elizabeth Hoy

- ☐ 996 PERCHANCE TO MARY
      Celine Conway
- ☐ 997 CASTLE THUNDERBIRD
      Susan Barrie
- ☐ 999 GREEN FINGERS FARM
      Joyce Dingwell
- ☐ 1014 HOUSE OF LORRAINE
      Rachel Lindsey
- ☐ 1027 THE LONELY SHORE
      Anne Weale
- ☐ 1223 THE GARDEN OF PERSEPHONE
      Nan Asquith
- ☐ 1245 THE BAY OF MOONLIGHT
      Rose Burghley
- ☐ 1319 BRITTLE BONDAGE
      Rosalind Brett

To: **HARLEQUIN READER SERVICE, Dept. N 401**
   M.P.O. Box 707, Niagara Falls, N.Y. 14302
   Canadian address: Stratford, Ont., Canada

☐ Please send me the free Harlequin Romance Catalogue.
☐ Please send me the titles checked.
   I enclose $_____ (No C.O.D.'s), All books are
   60c each. To help defray postage and handling cost,
   please add 25c.

Name _____

Address _____

City/Town _____

State/Prov. _____ Zip _____

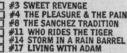